Now the ... Harl...
is comi...

One of our most po... ...mances ever,
Anne Mather's "Leopard in the Snow," is
now an unforgettable motion picture.
Look for it at a theater near you.

Harlequin Presents...

KEIR DULLEA · SUSAN PENHALIGON

Leopard in the Snow

Guest Stars
KENNETH MORE · BILLIE WHITELAW

featuring GORDON THOMSON as MICHAEL
and JEREMY KEMP as BOLT

Produced by JOHN QUESTED and CHRIS HARROP
Screenplay by ANNE MATHER and JILL HYEM
Directed by GERRY O'HARA

An Anglo-Canadian Co-Production

OTHER

Harlequin Romances

by ELIZABETH ASHTON

Many of these titles are available at your local bookseller
or through the Harlequin Reader Service.

For a free catalogue listing all available Harlequin Romances,
send your name and address to:

HARLEQUIN READER SERVICE,
M.P.O. Box 707, Niagara Falls, N.Y. 14302
Canadian address: Stratford, Ontario, Canada N5A 6W4

or use order coupon at back of books.

Green
Harvest

by

ELIZABETH ASHTON

Harlequin Books

TORONTO • LONDON • NEW YORK • AMSTERDAM • SYDNEY

Original hardcover edition published in 1977
by Mills & Boon Limited

ISBN 0-373-02116-X

Harlequin edition published November 1977

PRINTED IN U.S.A.

CHAPTER ONE

'AND this is Toni.'

Julian Everard freed himself from his mother's embrace and turned to introduce the child who was regarding them with solemn black eyes that concealed a spark of jealousy. Zio Giulio was her possession, the only anchor to which she had to cling since the disaster that had orphaned her, and already she was quick to resent anyone else who had a claim upon him.

'Come and kiss your aunt,' Julian went on, wishing she did not look so like a scared rabbit. Her black hair was scraped back unbecomingly behind her ears and her eyes looked enormous in her thin little face as she stared at mother and son apprehensively. She was deciding that she had been cheated. Julian had promised her she would find another mother in his, actually her great-aunt, but the elegant woman with her fine aristocratic features and still slim figure bore no resemblance to her own opulent parent, who like many Italians had grown stout in middle life. Mothers in Toni's limited experience were plump homely creatures with kind dark eyes. This woman's were grey and penetrating under her well dressed still blonde hair. Toni decided she did not look at all cosy, like Mamma had done.

'*Non desidero*,' she muttered.

Linda Everard raised her thin eyebrows.

'Can't she speak English?'

'Perfectly—Lewis ensured that. She's bi-lingual, she is his daughter.'

He had to keep reminding himself of that, for he

could see no trace of the Everards in his cousin's child. Lewis's outward seeming had been true Everard as he was himself, a type that had persisted through generations, tall and blond with keen blue eyes, vivid eyes without a hint of grey as so many blue eyes have. There the likeness ended, for Lewis had been a weakling, a failure, who dabbled unsuccessfully in art as a pretext to conceal his inadequacies. When his father had died, he had bought a small property in northern Italy with his patrimony and had eked out a hand-to-mouth existence with the aid of his wife who grew and marketed vegetables. About his marriage he had been secretive, and it was some time before he informed his family of it. He's ashamed of their poverty, Julian had thought when he visited them in the province of Fruili-Venezia prior to the catastrophe, and had felt a little guilty when he thought of his own comfortable circumstances. The lira notes he had passed surreptitiously to Maria with a murmured something about using them for the child had been accepted with unconcealed avidity. He had promised to call again upon his return from a climbing holiday in the Dolomites, none of them foreseeing what was to come. To the child Toni he had appeared as a young god with the sunlight in his hair, his bronzed limbs and ravishing smile. He had driven her into the nearest town in his hired car, that in itself a rare treat and bought her sweets and a doll, largesse which left her speechless. When he had left she had besought him:

'Come again, Zio Giulio.'

He promised he would, not knowing that he would be back within days when what the insurance companies term 'an act of God' had destroyed the whole district and all that was dear and familiar to poor Toni had been swept away, her own survival a miracle.

6

Julian had gone there at once as soon as the earth-quake was reported. Maria and Lewis were beyond all help, but Toni he rescued from the improvised refugee camp. Bewildered and shocked, she had clung to him. Though much younger than her father he was sufficiently like him for her to find him familiar.

He informed his mother that her nephew and his wife were dead, and that he proposed to bring Toni back with him eventually. Meanwhile there were certain formalities to be gone through, and he intended to spend some time with her at a homely Italian lakeside hotel, until she had recovered from the worst of her shock. There the friendly staff, aware of her tragedy, made much of her, and Julian with praiseworthy patience in a young man of twenty-five devoted all his time to her. She never mentioned her parents, but she bitterly mourned the loss of the doll he had given to her. That was easily replaced, the greater loss would be more difficult, but he hoped his parents would take her in. Linda had always regretted that she had only one child and beneath her somewhat austere exterior lay an unexpectedly warm heart. If she did not take to Toni the alternative was an orphanage, and that was unthinkable, so naturally he was anxious that the little girl should make a good impression, but Toni, with the contrariness of children, seemed determined to be unco-operative.

She was overawed by the big, low room, larger even than the lounge at the hotel, which had seemed vast to her after the tiny cottage that had housed her. But hotels, she knew, were holiday places built to accommodate many visitors. Could this huge room actually belong to a home—Julian's home—which he had assured her would be hers also? She could not visualise herself living among such grandeur. Living was cooking, washing and painting; she had already experimented with her father's watercolours, all done in the same confined space. But there were no signs of such activities here, and the tea table set out with china and silver looked too pretty for ordinary use.

Nor could she imagine Linda Everard in her elegant afternoon dress, with pearls at her throat, her fair hair, as yet untouched by grey, beautifully waved, her face skilfully made up, performing the chores that had been Maria's lot. Mamma was rarely seen without an apron, with her black hair escaping from its combs, but Mamma had been approachable. This self-contained woman was not.

Toni was suddenly assailed by a wave of homesickness. She longed for the stone-floored living room in the box of a cottage where she had spent her infancy, permeated by the familiar smell of garlic and dried herbs hanging from the ceiling. The windowsills had always been adorned with either laundry put out to dry, or bedding to air. Here the wide windows were draped with floor-length curtains, and the whole room appeared immaculate. The carpet beneath her feet, enclosed in sandals that felt stiff to one accustomed to run about barefoot, was thick and soft. It all seemed so strange and alien to her.

Once her father had taken her to Venice and they had gone over one of the ancient palaces. She was reminded of that experience, though Julian's home looked a good deal cleaner, but it had not occurred to her that modern people could reside in such surroundings. Historical characters had for her the same unreality as the images and pictures of the saints who lived in the churches in Italy.

Actually Linda had groomed herself carefully to welcome her son and had laid the afternoon tea in

8

what she still called the drawing room in his honour. Normally she and her husband used the much smaller morning room, which would have been a happier choice from Toni's point of view.

'Tony?' Linda queried doubtfully, surveying the small figure before her. 'But you said she was a girl, didn't you?' For the thin long-legged form in shorts and tee-shirt could have been of either sex.

This aspersion upon her femininity roused Toni into finding her voice.

'Antonia, Luisa Everard,' she announced shrilly.

Linda laughed. 'What a big name for such a small person! You're not much like your ...' She checked herself as Julian frowned warningly. He had noticed how Toni had flinched when he had tactlessly mentioned Lewis previously. Her loss was still too new for her to be able to bear references to her parents.

'... like us,' Linda concluded lamely.

'Her ... I mean she's partly Italian,' Julian reminded her.

Linda nodded comprehendingly, understanding why he had not mentioned Maria's name. She wondered what Lewis's wife had been like.

'Ah, yes, of course,' she said. 'You must tell me all about it later on. Your father won't be in until dinner, he had to go to Shrewsbury on business. Tea's all ready—I made it as soon as I saw the car coming up the drive. Come and sit beside me, on the sofa, Toni.' She put out her hand.

Toni shrank away from her, her dark eyes widening nervously. Overwhelmed by bashfulness, she turned to Julian, clutching his leg, and burying her face in his trousers.

'Come, come little one,' he coaxed her. 'You mustn't be shy. We're all family here.'

9

He gently disengaged her clinging arms and lifted her. Though Toni was eight years old, she was small for her age and much too underweight. He sat down on one of the easy chairs, holding her on his knees. Over her head he told his mother:

'Poor Toni is still suffering from shock and a plethora of new impressions. She ... er ... rather clings to me as the one person she knows.'

He smiled apologetically, a charming boyish smile, though Julian Everard was no longer a boy. Linda regarded him with frank amazement.

'Good heavens, Julian, this is a new role for you. I never thought of you as ... er ... paternal.'

His face registered almost comical dismay. 'Paternal —good God!' he ejaculated. 'It's just that ... Oh, I'll explain everything later on. Come, Toni, I can't drink my tea with you on my lap. Here!' He hooked a stool towards him with one foot. 'You can sit beside me.' He looked at the round tea-table set before his mother, the silver teapot brought out in his honour. 'I think some warm milk, if it's not too much trouble. Toni isn't used to tea yet.'

'Certainly. I'll ask Mrs Craddock to heat some.' Linda rose to her feet. 'I don't think she's gone home yet.' She was referring to her daily woman.

Left alone, Julian told the child, 'You mustn't be afraid of my mother, she wants to be kind to you.'

'She'll take you away from me,' Toni said stubbornly.

'Don't be silly, Toni, nobody can do that.' He hesitated; he had a job—should he warn her that she would be left with his mother without him? But he still had some vacation time left and he decided not to upset her further.

'Don't you think this is a nice room?' he went on.

'Whiteladies has been in our family for generations. It's a very old house.'

Toni lifted her head from his knee where she had laid it when he had put her upon the stool. She looked at the brick fireplace which accommodated logs in winter but was now filled with a Grecian vase containing great sprays of evergreen.

'Where do you cook?' she asked.

'In the kitchen, of course.'

Toni's eyes widened. 'Do you have a kitchen as well as this?'

He laughed. 'And a dining room, a morning room and bedrooms, to say nothing of the gardens, farm buildings and fields.'

Toni shook her head in bewilderment.

'It's all too big.'

'You'll get used to it, and you'll help to fill it.'

He became silent, recalling his mother's frequent plaint that their family was so limited. His father had married late in life and there had only been himself at Whiteladies after Lewis had gone to Italy. His uncle, Lewis's father, had married young, and for a long time had believed himself and his son to be the heirs presumptive. It had been a blow to him when his elder brother had married Linda and produced a child. He had died shortly afterwards of a coronory and his wife had married again. Lewis went abroad and was not heard of for some years. The Everards were neither long-lived nor prolific in offspring. Julian's parents were always urging him to marry and carry on the line, but his father had been nearly double his age before he did so and Julian saw no reason why he should hasten to forgo his liberty.

Linda returned with the glass of warm milk enclosed in a plastic holder and Antonia instantly became dumb. To Mrs Everard's kindly questions she either shook her head or whispered 'Non capisco.' Her dark eyes had the wary look of a suspicious animal. Her elders forbore to rebuke her, both understanding she was tired and overwrought. Mother and son chatted, she giving him the local news, he describing details of his holiday. Of the subject uppermost in their thoughts they could not speak before the child.

Toni sipped the milk and was persuaded to attempt a sandwich. She left half of it and her head began to nod.

'I think bed,' Mrs Everard suggested.

'Where have you put her?'

'In the dressing room between your room and mine. I thought she'd be lost in the guest room. Can she put herself to bed?'

'I'd better go up with her. I ... well, I've been acting nannie with the help of the chambermaid.'

Linda laughed. 'You poor dear, but surely I can relieve you now?'

'I was hoping you would, but this first night ... everything must seem very strange to her.'

'Of course. A bath might relax her.'

'She'll like that, with my assistance.'

Linda raised her brows but made no comment. She accompanied them upstairs, Julian carrying Toni, her arms about his neck nearly throttling him. The room allocated to her was reassuringly small, a slit between the two larger ones on either side, but the bathroom was another matter; she had never become accustomed to the one at the hotel with its mysterious plumbing. At home she had been bathed in a tub in front of the fire with spring water warmed by a contribution from the kettle. The Whiteladies bathroom was a miracle of gleaming mirrors and shining taps. Julian ran a bath

12

for her, while Linda stripped off her scanty clothing and wrapped her in a towel. He discreetly withdrew and Toni's face puckered as if she were about to cry, but Linda quickly diverted her with a cascade of coloured bath salts into the water and the promise that Julian would come and say goodnight to her.

Smelling of lavender, her dark hair sprayed over the pillow, Toni watched the door anxiously until he came in. As he bent over her, she seized his hand and clung to it.

'Where will you be?'

'Not far away.' He indicated the door between them. 'But you'll be asleep when I come up.'

'Don't go.'

He sat down on the bed. 'I'll stay for a little while, but you must go to sleep.'

An owl hooted in a tree outside and Toni started up trembling.

'What was that?'

'Only an owl, darling. Didn't you have them in Italy? They're night birds.'

'I know, Daddy showed me pictures . . .' Her face contorted. 'You'll be my daddy now?'

'Well, not exactly, but I'll always take care of you, Toni,' he promised rashly, anxious to comfort her. She gave a long sigh, but she still clung to his hand.

'Tell me a story,' she coaxed.

Julian was not much of a raconteur, but since taking charge of Toni he had dredged up the half forgotten fairy tales of his own nursery days. He embarked upon Goldilocks and the Three Bears.

'Once upon a time there was a little girl with golden hair and blue eyes . . .'

'Like you,' Toni interrupted.

'Yes, well, don't put me off my stroke, child.'

The story proceeded until the dark eyes closed. Julian gently withdrew his hand and stood up, looking down at the small black head upon the pillow, her long lashes like fans upon her cheeks, with an expression none of his business colleagues would have recognised. He was considered by them to be something of a 'tough guy.' His work being concerned with petrochemistry and energy economics, he had spent a year on an oil rig to gain practical experience—a hardening process. His aim was to qualify for a post abroad. He contrived to disguise an underlying tenderness towards all weak and helpless creatures to which Toni had appealed, but he would not allow her to become an encumbrance. Children were resilient and in the shelter of his home with Linda ready to mother her she would soon recover from the trauma of her recent experiences and he would have no further responsibility for her.

Linda unleashed a spate of questions as soon as he joined her. She was not wholly ignorant of Lewis's circumstances. About the time of Toni's birth she had received a letter from him saying that his wife was about to have a baby, business was bad, few people, even tourists, were ready to buy paintings and could she oblige with a temporary loan? Linda sent what she knew would amount to a gift, followed by subsequent 'loans', which were never repaid. She did not tell her husband, who considered Lewis to be a wastrel and a scrounger, but the mention of a baby had softened her. Lewis was never very expansive about his family, he merely stated that both his wife and child were well. When Julian planned to spend a holiday in the Dolomites, she begged him to look them up and discover their true circumstances, which he did.

When the awful catastrophe occurred and the whole

14

district was laid waste, he found Toni numb with shock and almost distraught, but she remembered him and clung to him with passionate adoration. She could not bear him out of her sight, and at the small hotel she slept in an alcove in his room. She had nightmares, when she woke sobbing with terror and only the shelter of his arms could cause the shuddering to stop. His assurances that he would take her to his mother who loved children and would compensate her for her loss left her cold. She only wanted to be with Julian.

The records pertaining to Antonia Luisa Everard had been lost in the devastation of the countryside, which was perhaps as well, for Julian had a suspicion that his lackadaisical cousin had not married his Italian *contadina* until Toni's advent made it desirable. In fact she was so unlike the blond Everards with her black hair and matt white skin, he wondered if she were really Lewis's child at all. But his cousin had accepted her as such and Julian did not mention his doubt to his mother, for he did not want to prejudice her against the orphan. Linda had a strong clannish sense, hence her help to Lewis, but she might jib at a child of unknown parentage. During their sojourn in Italy Toni had crept into his heart, she was such a pathetic little scrap, and if he had been older he might have considered adopting her himself. But he did not want any ties before he must assume them, for his father was growing old and he would eventually have to run Whiteladies for him.

Edgar Everard came in during Julian's recital and confirmed that he and his wife would certainly bring up the child.

'Though I hope she turns out better than Lewis did,' he said. 'That boy was never any good. Thank God

15

you came along, Julian, and stopped his chance of inheriting Whiteladies.'

'Which he couldn't do now, poor blighter, even if I died,' Julian said sombrely.

'Pity Antonia isn't a boy,' Linda sighed. 'Then she could have carried on the name if you don't marry, but of course you will, dear boy.'

'Oh, don't be so feudal,' Julian told her impatiently. 'All that sort of thing died out with the dodo, and poor Whiteladies is a bit of an anachronism, and will be soon too expensive to run.'

He sighed in his turn, for though he had no intention of settling there for a long while to come he had a strong feeling for his ancestral home.

'These damn taxes!' Edgar exploded, and they proceeded to discuss politics.

Time passed. Toni gradually became resigned to her new way of life, so different from the carefree existence in Italy. She had gone to a convent school, but her attendance was spasmodic. The Everards intended to send her to a good boarding school eventually where she would have young companionship. Meanwhile, finding how backward she was, they engaged a retired schoolmistress to coach her. Toni was intelligent and learned easily, but chafed at the long hours she must spend indoors studying. As compensation, Julian bought her a pony and taught her to ride. He, to her great grief, went to work in London, but he always returned for the weekends. It was only then that she seemed to come alive, and he devoted all his time to her, much to his mother's chagrin, who was always hoping he would show some interest in a nice girl with the intention of marrying her. Julian, with the prospect of assignations abroad as soon as he was fully qualified, was determined not to become involved. Toni presented no threat to his independence.

'She can't be any real company for you,' Linda pointed out. 'She's only a child.'

'But a very bright one,' he returned. 'I'm amazed at how much she has assimilated since she came here. Every time I come home, she seems a little more ... um ... civilised. Besides, she still needs reassurance.'

'Surely I can give her that?'

'In time, Mother.' He frowned. He was disappointed that Toni had not taken to Linda. When he tackled her about it, she told him:

'Zia Linda,' for so she called her, the Italian form seemed less stiff, 'doesn't really like me. She thinks I'm odd. I can't help it, I know I don't look like an English girl, it's because of Mamma. You're the only person who cares what becomes of me.'

Julian denied this statement vehemently to conceal the faint suspicion that she spoke the truth.

They were out riding in the early morning, for it was midsummer and the day promised to be hot. They had stopped at their favourite haunt, a meadow crossed by a meandering stream over which willow trees hung. Toni looked up adoringly at Julian's brown face, the new sunlight turning his hair to silver-gilt. She thought he looked like a Greek hero, a trite comparison, but she had been studying Greek mythology.

'Let's stay here a little,' Julian said, swinging out of his saddle, 'we'll go down to the stream.'

Toni dismounted and they tied their horses to the gate. Entering by the stile at its side, they wandered through an ocean of buttercups and daisies towards the water.

Reverting to the subject of Mrs Everard, Toni said:

'Zia Linda doesn't like you spending so much time with me.'

'Good lord, why shouldn't I?'

'Because I'm a child, and even if I were older, I'm not eli ... eligible,' she stumbled over the long word. She slanted an upward glance to his face. 'I'm not stupid, Zio Giulio. She thinks Miss Grayson would be a more suitable companion for you. She wants you to marry her.'

In anything that affected Julian, Toni had almost uncanny divination; besides, she often overheard remarks not intended for her ears. She watched Julian's expression anxiously for any change, wondering if he liked Miss Grayson, who always ignored herself.

Julian laughed, switching idly at a buttercup with his riding crop. His expression was derisive and Toni's heart lightened.

'No, thank you! She's too liberated for my taste and much too managing. When I marry, if I marry, I'd prefer something soft and feminine. There'll be no doubt about who's the boss in my house, whatever Women's Lib have to say.'

Toni thrilled to that touch of masculine arrogance, the Latin in her reacting to male dominance. Approaching her teens now, she was both physically and mentally in advance of an English girl of her years by reason of her Italian blood. She said insinuatingly:

'If you're in no hurry, I'll be ever so soft and feminine when I'm grown up.'

'My pet, by the time you're marriageable I'll be an old man.'

'*Sciocchezza!*' She waved a slim brown hand and went on earnestly: 'A man ought to be older than his wife. They mostly were in Italy. He has to have a home

18

to offer her, and you'll have Whiteladies which we both love.'

Julian smiled indulgently, amused by her quaint air of worldly wisdom.

'You may grow out of that. Most young people want something more lively. You'll have changed very much by the time you're adult.'

'I'm sure I shan't.'

'Believe me, you will. Another ten years and you won't know yourself.'

'Ten years!' She looked dismayed and added inconsequently: 'Juliet was married when she was fourteen.'

'Juliet was a fictitious person, and she wasn't much to be envied. According to English law you can't marry until you're sixteen, and that's much too young. I hope you won't rush into matrimony, Toni, not until you've learned something about life. Make sure you pick the right person.'

She had already done that and was certain she would never change. Her firm little chin set obstinately, but she said no more. They had reached the banks of the stream and they sat down upon a fallen tree, watching the swirling water. A dragonfly darted across it, an iridescent flash of blue. Julian glanced at her still profile anxiously. He had news to break to her which he feared would upset her. She turned her head and looked at him inquiringly, her intuition aware of some inner jubilation in him. Something had happened to please him very much.

The sun was gaining strength, sucking up the dew, and all about them was the tranquillity of pastoral England. He was loth to break its serenity, and hers, with his tidings. Instead he said:

'Incidentally, you might drop the Zio stuff. I'm not your uncle, I'm your cousin, once removed to be precise, and you're old enough now to call me Julian un-adorned.'

He could not have pleased her more. Cousins could marry, and that removal made them still less akin.

'Certainly, Giulio—I mean Julian,' she said demurely.

'That's better. You'd better forget your Italian—nobody understands it here and it makes you seem alien.'

She gave a small sigh. 'It's not easy to fit in. Sometimes I feel this life isn't real and I'll wake up in the cottage with Mamma and Papa and find it was all a dream.'

'But you've got over that? You're not unhappy?' he asked anxiously.

'I'll never be unhappy while I've got you,' she declared. 'And if it was all a dream I'd never have met you nor had my pony. I love Polly, and you bought her for me.'

He laughed. 'You seem to regard me as the provider of good things, but I'm sure my father would have given you a pony if I hadn't.'

She let it go at that. Already her feminine intuition was acute and she sensed her admission of dependence upon him had embarrassed him.

He glanced at her pale face that never seemed to gain much colour, the sheen of her hair smoothly parted in the centre and knotted in her nape. The open neck of her shirt showed the delicate lines of her throat and the base of her neck.

'You've improved a lot, Toni, by the time you leave school all the boys in the countryside will be after you.'

She turned to him with wide beseeching eyes.

'Must I go away to school, Julian? I mean ... what'll happen to Polly if I'm not here?'

'Of course you must go to school, but you'll come back here for holidays and Polly can be put out to grass while you're away.'

A select girls' boarding school at Church Stretton had been chosen for her and Julian was contributing towards the high fees.

'You'll enjoy it once you've got used to it,' he added.

'I'll hate it. A pack of giggling silly girls,' she said fiercely. Then she smiled impishly. 'But I'll have to pass the entrance exam. I'm sure I'll fail.'

'I don't think you will. I'm told Miss What's-her-name who has been tutoring you is very pleased with your progress.'

She flashed him a rebellious glance but said nothing. If she made no effort to pass she would fail. Interpreting her mood, Julian said gently:

'You must do your best, little one. It's very important to have a good education and it's a great opportunity to gain a place in such an exclusive school. There they'll teach you how to behave in polite society, the rather absurd conventions of your aunt's circle. You wouldn't want to disgrace us, would you?'

Toni gazed meditatively down at the stream. A family of ducks went sailing past, a trail of half-fledged youngsters following their parents. Julian would one day be master of Whiteladies, he would require a wife who was accustomed to social usages to act as his hostess to his friends and manage his household. She would need training before she could hold her own among the county families. Her rebellion died and resolution took its place. She would allow herself to be groomed and educated if it was to be a means to attain what she most desired.

'Then I shall pass,' she announced. 'I'm going to make you proud of me, Julian.'

21

'That's the spirit!' He nodded approval.

'But I'll miss you so,' she wailed. 'You'll come and see me?'

He shook his head. 'I'm afraid that won't be possible. I'm going away too.' A note of excitement crept into his voice. 'I've been offered a job in Saudi Arabia. At last I'm going abroad.'

'Oh no!' Toni whispered. The bright sunlight seemed to darken about her and the stream wavered before her eyes.

'I'm afraid it's Oh yes, darling. It's what I've wanted and I've worked hard all these years to qualify for it. Now I'm about the right age with no ties to speak of, I was accepted at once.'

'How long will you be away?'

He hesitated. 'Quite a while, I'm afraid.'

'How long exactly?' she insisted.

'Well, three to four years.'

'*Dio mio!*' To Toni it seemed an eternity, as long as she had been at Whiteladies, and during those years her life in Italy had become remote. She could not bear the thought that Julian also might recede, like the memories of her parents. Her great eyes were tragic.

'Darling, don't look like that,' Julian besought her. 'The time will soon pass and you'll become absorbed in your school life. The happiest years, they say they are.'

Purgatory, Toni thought how shall I endure them? But she realised what this assignment meant to him and with a wintry smile she managed to say bravely:

'I'm awfully glad for your sake.'

'Thank you, darling. You'll write of course. I'd like a weekly letter, if it isn't too much of a drag, telling me all your doings. I'll be most interested in your progress.'

'Oh yes, yes, it won't be a drag at all,' she cried eagerly. 'And you'll write to me?'

'When I've time, but you won't find petrochemistry and energy marketing very interesting.'

'Everything you do interests me,' she declared emphatically. 'And I want to hear about the country and the people you meet.'

Would there be other girls out there? she wondered. Other oil men might take their families, but surely the supply of eligible young women would be limited?

'I shan't have much time for social contacts,' Julian told her. 'I'm dedicated to my work.'

Which was reassuring. 'I'll be quite grown up when you come back,' she observed.

'Well, hardly, but I hope you'll still be my Toni,' he returned, with more warmth than wisdom.

'Then and always,' she vowed fervently.

At least he would be leaving Miss Grayson behind.

CHAPTER TWO

TONI passed her entrance examination with ease and duly went to Greystones School. Linda Everard had chosen it because she had been a pupil there and had a high opinion of the type of girl it turned out, and hoped her great-niece could be moulded into the same pattern. The girl was shy and gauche with strangers and her attempts to introduce her to friends' children were a complete failure. Toni simply did not mix.

Miss Selby, the headmistress, was sympathetic and was certain the atmosphere of Greystones would have the desired effect. It was not a strict establishment and Toni would not be burdened with too many regulations. She made a point of studying each pupil's individual needs.

Sport figured largely in the curriculum, which would help to engender the team spirit which it seemed necessary Antonia should acquire. She also encouraged any particular talent a girl showed. Linda hoped Toni would not develop an interest in art, which had proved so unsatisfactory in her father's case. That Toni had an artistic bent, but in another direction, was yet to be discovered.

Greystones was an old manor house that had been converted into a school. It was situated on the outskirts of a small Shropshire town, and was a charming place with its own swimming pool and tennis courts. Toni had no fault to find with the layout and she showed an aptitude for tennis, but unfortunately for Linda's hopes, she persisted in holding aloof from the other girls, whom she secretly despised. Their conversation and interests seemed to her so trivial. The tragedy that had overwhelmed her so early in her life set her apart. Mrs Everard's suggestion that she should bring a little friend home for the holidays was met by a polite negative. Toni made no friends.

Julian had gone to Saudi Arabia. Her parting with him had been almost formal, because his parents were there and Toni would not betray her heartbreak in their presence, but she had watched his car disappear down the drive with a heart that felt like lead. For the next few days she moved and spoke like an automaton, and when Linda tried to comfort her, she said coldly that Julian had his own life to lead and she had hers, and he had wanted to leave them.

Baffled, Mrs Everard retreated, saying Antonia was quite incomprehensible, she seemed to have no feelings. She herself was bitterly disappointed that Miss Grayson's charms had been unable to captivate her son. Polly the pony could have told a different story, if she could

24

speak. Only with her did Toni give way to her grief, and the pony's mane was plentifully bedewed with her tears. Leaving her was a further wrench when she was packed off to Greystones, but she would be seeing her again in the holidays.

Dutifully she wrote to Julian every week, the composition of these letters being her one real pleasure. His replies were infrequent and when she received one she read it and re-read it until the thin paper was worn to shreds. They were her lifeline in an existence that was a kind of limbo until he came again.

She found one outlet for her repressed emotions. Drama and speech training were part of the school's recreational programme, and Toni revealed an unsuspected talent in this direction. She declaimed Alfred Noyes' 'The Highwayman' with much tragic intensity at one of the school concerts. Her teacher was delighted with her and let her learn some of the great dramatic speeches of literature, Andromache's farewell to her little son from *The Trojan Women*, and Juliet's potion scene being among them. Juliet, who had married at fourteen and brought about her husband's and her own death. Toni fairly revelled in them, finding in these fictitious woes her own release.

In her last year she made a friend. Annabel Thorne had been sent to Greystones to complete her education and was put into Toni's form. A red-haired extrovert, she was immediately attracted by the dark silent girl so different from herself, and refusing to be snubbed set herself to draw her out. Little by little Toni yielded to her advances and began to enjoy her company. Mrs Thorne was a retired actress and Annabel entertained her with racy stories about the stage.

'Mother thinks you've got a marvellous face and voice for drama,' Annabel told Toni after one of her parent's visits when she had introduced her to her friend. 'Ever thought of being an actress, Toni?'

'No, never,' Toni said firmly. That was not the sort of future she wanted, but she had not confided to Annabel her fixation upon Julian. It was something too intimate and sacred to divulge to anyone.

That Christmas term Miss Selby embarked upon a dramatic production instead of the usual concert. Annabel was cast as Celia and Toni as Rosalind in *As You Like It*. The minor roles were all to be played by the girls, but a trio of carefully vetted youths from the local drama group were invited to play Orlando, the Duke and Jacques, Miss Selby hoping to leaven her large feminine lump with a touch of masculinity. All three promptly fell in love with Toni, and in the part of vivacious Rosalind she was quite entrancing. The young men were not supposed to fraternise with the girls off stage, which led to a great deal of intrigue to circumvent the surveillance of the mistresses. Notes were pressed into willing hands, during rehearsals, attempts were made to meet in the corners on the sly, for as Toni remained inaccessible, the lovelorn swains had to console themselves with easier prey. Toni ignored them completely, which her Orlando found difficult to reconcile with her charming coquetry when playing her part. But as the production advanced she unbent towards him, for he reminded her a little of Julian; he had the same colouring and boyish smile. They had many scenes together, but to his insistent requests that she would meet him outside the school she continued to be adamant.

'If I was caught I'd be expelled,' she pointed out.

'You could manage not to be caught. You're not a goody-goody, are you, Toni? You look full of mischief in the play.'

'My education is important to me,' she returned. 'I won't do anything to jeopardise it.'

What would Julian say if she were sent home for meeting a youth illicitly? It was unthinkable to contemplate running such a risk, and certainly not for Orlando, to whom she was completely indifferent.

'You've got everything,' Annabel told her a little enviously. 'Looks, poise, sex-appeal. What are you going to do with it all?'

Toni laughed and shrugged her shoulders.

'You flatter me, Anna, but I've no plans. I'll probably vegetate at Whiteladies looking after my aunt and uncle.'

And waiting for Julian, hoping he'll find me as attractive as this other boy does, she thought wistfully. Annabel's compliments heartened her enormously. When Julian returned he would find she had blossomed into beauty and he could no longer treat her as a child, as from the tone of his letters he still considered her to be. She described her part in the play, saying she wished he could see it. He replied that he did too; Christmas always made him feel nostalgic, but by next Christmas he expected to be home. He hoped to be back by midsummer and he had several months leave due to him, news that sent her spirits sky-rocketing.

As You Like It is all about love. Silvius the shepherd describes the emotion at some length in iambic pentameter, 'All adoration, duty and observance', which described her own feelings. Parents and other relatives were invited to the performance. Linda came, and Annabel's mother. Toni's Rosalind was a triumph. In her acting she was able to release the repressions which normally bound her, she became a different person on stage, aglow with gaiety and vitality. Her interpretation was curiously mature, and whereas the others were

27

obviously schoolgirls, she appeared adult.

Mrs Thorne was delighted by her performance. Though she had given up the stage when she married she still retained many friends in the profession. She told Linda that Toni was quite exceptional and ought to make acting her career.

'I could help her,' she said. 'I've still got some influence.'

Mrs Everard thanked her politely but was not enthusiastic. She had old-fashioned notions about the stage and did not want her great-niece involved with it. She was sure Julian would not approve either. Nor did Toni express any wish in this connection, to Annabel's astonishment.

'Good gracious, Toni, if I had got half what you've got there'd be no holding me,' she declared. 'What are you going to do with your life? You can't mean to bury yourself on that ... that farm!'

'Whiteladies is more than a farm,' Toni returned serenely. 'I'm waiting to see what turns up.'

Which meant Julian and her belief that he would claim her.

Edgar Everard did not come to see the play, he said school Shakespeare was more than he could face. Linda told him he had missed something.

'Toni was incredible,' she said. 'So alive. I've been in despair about her—she didn't seem human, like an icicle. Oh, she's always tractable and her manners are pleasant, but I never feel I can get near her. Her performance was a revelation.'

Edgar found his graceful teenage niece very nice to look at and he liked her air of deference towards him, so he defended her, saying:

'She did have an awful experience, the complete

destruction of her childhood's world. It was bound to leave some mark.'

'But she was only eight, she should be over that now,' Linda declared.

Early impressions may become overlaid but they are never wholly eradicated, but stronger than the trauma of that calamity was Toni's obsession with Julian. He had come to deliver her when her world was in ruins, saving possibly her life and certainly her reason. She did not believe the bond between them could ever be broken. Yet she had her moments of unease. Julian was popular with women and he was not unsusceptible. In spite of what he had said he had flirted a little with Miss Grayson. Toni studied his epistles, which were usually full of descriptions of the places he visited, seeking a hint of a romantic attachment. There never was one, though he occasionally mentioned a girl by name. There was a Miss Jessamine Boycott who was working as a secretary to some oil magnate whom he had met at a dinner. 'Nice to see a fresh English face,' he wrote, 'but she was quite ordinary.' Toni dismissed her as unimportant.

Winter passed into spring and spring to summer, and at last Julian gave her the date of his arrival and said he would come to visit her at school.

That night she studied her face in the bathroom mirror, the only place where she could be sure of privacy, with critical eyes. Her reflection showed an ebon and ivory beauty framed in a cloud of dark hair, black level eyebrows above large lustrous eyes set off by the matt skin inherited from her mother. Only the redness of her passionate mouth gave her a touch of colour. Her well shaped head was supported by a slender graceful body. She was not vain, but she would have been stupid not to be aware that she possessed a strange wistful beauty, and Toni was not stupid, she only valued her looks in connection with their effect upon Julian. Was she too exotic-looking? she wondered anxiously. He had mentioned Miss Jessamine Boycott's fresh English face. Would she appear to him too like the dark Arab beauties he had left behind him? But those stupid boys in the play had admired her, regarded her as an attractive young woman. Could she win for herself the reciprocation that she so desperately desired?

She frequently heard whenever she was at White-ladies Linda's expressed hopes that Julian 'would find a nice girl' to marry and be content to settle down at home and produce the grandchildren for which she yearned, a wish fully supported by her husband. That Toni might attract him had never occurred to them. They regarded the gap in years to be too great for her to interest him. They still saw her as a child. But Toni was growing fast out of adolescence. Helped by her Latin blood, she was ripe for love, but there never had and never would be anyone for her except Julian.

The girls were playing tennis when Julian arrived. Toni glimpsed him out of the corner of her eye. A few years back, she would have flung down her racquet and rushed to greet him, but a new shyness and sense of her own dignity caused her to restrain the impulse. Some instinct prompted her to finish the game. It wanted only two points to win the set. Suddenly it seemed important to her to win, an omen of success in a much greater venture. She was serving, and her first ball went over the net fast and sure, impossible to return, and her opponents did not try. Vantage in, she was nearly there. She walked sedately across to serve her next ball, never raising her eyes towards Julian, apparently unaware of his presence, though she was conscious of him in every nerve. Her service was returned, but her partner slammed it down from the net where she was standing. Game and set. She smiled at her opponents, and swinging her racquet walked towards the two spectators, outward serenity masking her inner tumult. Her partner, after uttering a whoop of triumph, made herself scarce.

Miss Selby had told Julian; 'Antonia is good at games.'

He made no response as he watched the white-clad figure in regulation tennis dress reach to deliver her services. Grace and power were an irresistable combination. His eyes were full of admiration as she walked towards him with her long lithe stride. She was taking stock of him; he had not changed except for the sun wrinkles round his eyes, eyes still piercingly blue, the more so because of his deep tan. The sunlight found golden glints in his fair hair, except for the forelock which was blanched flaxen. He wore it short, 'More hygenic in hot countries,' he declared. Like many blond men he did not age perceptibly and sports kept him fit; he had not succumbed to the figure-ruining habit of too many iced drinks.

Within a few paces of him, Toni halted, overcome by shyness, and he smiled, his teeth very white in his brown face.

'Those were two excellent shots,' he told her, 'worthy of Wimbledon. Congratulations on winning the set.'

She hung her head, still speechless, and he went on:

'I hope you're pleased to see me.'

'Oh, Julian!' she breathed, raising her head, a faint flush creeping into her pale cheeks; Toni never tanned very much. Her eyes were more eloquent than her tongue. Julian realised with a sense of shock that she was beautiful. They stood gazing at each other, oblivious of the watchful Miss Selby. She clicked her tongue, looking from one to the other of their conscious

31

faces. She was dimly aware of a current of emotion passing between them, all the more potent because it had no outward expression. This still young-looking man had been talking to her as if Toni were still a child in whom he took an avuncular interest, but he was actually her cousin, and not in the first degree. She could see he was impressed by the enormous improvement in his protégée, but was that all? As for Toni, her luminous eyes betrayed her. Miss Selby shrugged her shoulders; their subsequent history was no affair of hers, and Antonia had always been something of a problem child.

'I've come to take you out,' Julian said at length. 'Miss Selby has given her permission. I thought we might have tea somewhere.'

'I . . . I must go and change.' Toni looked down at her abbreviated dress, thus directing Julian's glance to her long, shapely legs.

'Of course, run along,' Miss Selby bade her briskly. 'I'll entertain Mr Everard while you do so.'

'I'll be as quick as I can,' Toni promised, and sped away towards the school buildings. Outwardly she showed little sign of the welter of emotion into which she had been plunged. Julian was actually there, looking exactly as she had remembered him, and she had seen admiration in his eyes. Their brief exchange had been banal in the extreme, but how could it be anythink else in the presence of her headmistress? Soon they would be alone and he would praise her for the progress she had made, tell her how he had missed her and she would insist that they never must be parted again. If he wanted to go back to Saudi Arabia he could take her with him, she did not care in what capacity, but until she had seen him again she had not realised how utterly destitute she was without him.

Meanwhile Miss Selby was discussing her with Julian.

The girl was very intelligent, but she had shown no interest in any paticular career. She should be trained for something. Had he any plans for her? Julian was still suffering from the shock of discovering that little Toni had become a young woman. He had never considered what was to become of her. Vaguely he imagined that she would live at Whiteladies until she married someone in the locality.

'Does she show any aptitude for anything specially?' he asked.

'No. She's keen on horses, but you wouldn't want to make a groom of her. She shows a considerable dramatic talent. She was most impressive in our school play, but the stage is so overcrowded, besides ...' She shrugged her shoulders. The Everards she was sure would not approve of an acting career for Toni. 'She's not good with people.'

'What do you mean by that, Miss Selby?'

'She's always so withdrawn, as if she lived in another world.'

'Perhaps that's the artistic temperament,' Julian suggested, recalling that Lewis had been an artist, though not a very good one.

'Artistic fiddlesticks, that's an excuse for laziness,' Miss Selby said tartly. 'But Antonia isn't lazy, it's simply that she needs direction for her energies.'

'Perhaps she could learn shorthand and typing?' hazarded Julian, who had not much notion of professions for women.

Miss Selby looked at him severely. 'I can hardly visualise Antonia in an office,' she said drily.

'Well, since I'm taking her out this afternoon I'll see if I can discover her inclinations,' Julian told her. 'Young people are usually very definite about wanting

33

to do their own thing, as they put it, and live their own lives. Isn't that the jargon?'

Miss Selby looked at him pityingly. More perceptive than he was, she had an inkling of what Toni's 'thing' was, but that he would have to find out for himself.

Toni had changed into green slacks and a thin green tank top, the colour enhancing her ebony and ivory beauty. Her heavy hair was rolled into a knot at the nape of her neck, thus revealing the elegant shape of her head and the lovely lines of her jaw and throat. Julian's car was parked before the front entrance to the school and he was standing in the entrance hall, never used by the pupils, still chatting to Miss Selby when she came to join them. As Toni came towards them, Julian appraised her costume in one swift glance, and a gleam of approval showed in his eyes. She was like a wood-nymph, a dryad, sylphlike in her graceful movements. He thought he saw what Miss Selby meant when she said she was out of this world.

He remarked prosaically: 'She does you credit, Miss Selby.'

'We've done our best for her,' the schoolmistress returned. She considered the girl was too exotic-looking to be quite respectable. That dense black hair, those huge dark eyes with their plethora of lashes caused her to look out of place among the English girls who comprised the bulk of her scholars, daughters of county families and hunting squires, the few that were left with money. Heaven alone knew what the Everards could make of this wild poppy in their field of orthodox corn.

'Come along.' Julian linked his arm through Toni's. Over his shoulder he added, 'Goodbye, Miss Selby. I'll bring her back some time this evening.'

'We have supper at seven-thirty,' Miss Selby called

34

after them. 'Antonia knows that if she's late she goes without.'

'Quoth the dragon,' Julian murmured, his eyes meeting Toni's alight with laughter. He opened the car door for her. 'Where do you want to go?'

'Could we go up the Long Mynd?' she asked eagerly.

'I don't see why not. You like hills?'

He slid in beside her, as Toni said she did. Actually she was indifferent to where they went so long as she was with him, but since he had given her a choice she asked for the place she was seldom able to visit because of its difficult approach. The other girls disliked the steep climb and she was not permitted to go alone.

The road was winding and narrow with a deep drop on one side to the Carding Mill Valley far below. The bracken, since it was a hot summer, was burned to a russet brown, the ling, not yet in bloom, a purplish madder. The hill was not very high and rounded in shape, but it was steep. On the top there was a wide stretch of moorland, reaching to the horizon before it descended on the further side. Church Stretton was visible through a cleft in the moor, a cluster of buildings among the trees.

Julian stopped the car and they got out. The sun beat hotly down on the shadeless slopes, but Julian was used to heat and Toni delighted in it. A few sheep came up hopefully, having learned that visitors in cars often had scraps.

'Scroungers,' Julian remarked. 'No, we've nothing for you, so you can take yourselves off.'

The animals looked at them with avid eyes, then discovering that he spoke the truth ambled disgustedly away.

Julian and Toni walked over the heather. They climbed a humped knoll with a rocky outcrop at its summit upon which they seated themselves. All around them were the smooth-contoured hills with their steep declivities streaked with golden bracken amid the grass and heather. Overhead a lark sang. Julian slid from his perch and stretched himself full length on a smooth patch of turf.

'It's good to be back,' he sighed contentedly.

'Then don't go away again,' Toni urged. 'Why should you?'

'To please my firm, and I'm a bit young to vegetate. On the other hand, my father has aged a lot. It's hardly fair to leave him without help, perhaps one more tour before I become a farmer, though the old man doesn't seem to realise it mayn't be possible to keep Whiteladies after they're gone ...' He rambled on, more to himself than to her. Toni sat above him, her dark eyes very soft as she surveyed his recumbent figure. There was no superfluous flesh upon him, he was still as lean and agile as a youth. Suddenly he sat up.

'That's enough about me. Miss Selby was talking to me about you. What are you going to do with your life?'

Taken aback by his abrupt question, Toni stammered:

'I ... I don't know. Can't I live at Whiteladies?'

'But don't you want a career, to do your own thing, as the youngsters say? You should train for something. You can't shut yourself up at Whiteladies with an ageing family. You need young society.'

Nervously she pulled at a tuft of grass.

'I don't ... really I don't. I only want to be with you.'

There was a short silence. Toni bent her head, aware that he was looking at her intently through narrowed eyes. Then he smiled.

'That's very sweet of you, but suppose I decide to marry?'

Toni lifted her head, her eyes wide and appealing.

'Couldn't you marry me?'

Startled, Julian exclaimed; 'But, darling, you're much too young. You're what ... sixteen? Why, you hardly know you're born and I ... I'm over thirty. You need a boy of your own age.'

A suggestion Toni furiously repudiated. 'Boys are stupid and callow,' she declared. 'Oh, Julian, I've loved you ever since I first saw you. There'll never be anyone but you, and if you send me away I ... I'll die!'

She looked so tragic, Julian nearly laughed, but restrained himself in time. She must have some sort of fixation, but it could create a difficult situation, the more so because now he was becoming aware of her attraction as a woman. Those great dark eyes brimming with emotion, her matt skin and so black hair were enticing. Toni had fulfilled her promise to be soft and feminine, she was the essence of alluring womanhood.

Toni sensed some subtle change in him and guided by her instincts, she flung herself down upon him, her arms encircling his neck, pressing her young body against his lean muscular strength. Automatically his arms closed round her as he sank back in the heather, overborne by her sudden onslaught.

'Julian, I love you so,' she murmured, as her loosened hair fell about them like a veil. Their lips met. All about them was the sensuous slumbrous magic of the summer day, the murmur of the honey-seeking bees in the heather, the occasional bleat of a sheep. Toni's innocent abandonment was having the result for which she had hoped, as Julian's kisses became more ardent and she could feel the throb of his heart beneath her own, but after the first shock, he recovered himself.

Gently he disengaged himself from her clinging arms and sat up. She lay beside him, her hair around her like a shining web, her eyes closed, her whole body an invitation.

'This is madness,' he said hoarsely. 'You're a witch, Toni, but good lord, you mustn't be so ... er ... impulsive, my pet. It's dangerous.'

He rose to his feet, moved a few paces away and stood with his back to her, his clenched hands thrust into his trouser pockets.

Realising he had withdrawn, Toni opened her eyes and stared at his uncompromising back. Her pulses still throbbed from the torrent of emotion that had swept through her, but why had Julian gone away from her? She knew instinctively that she had aroused him, so why did he not take what she had offered? She raised herself on one elbow.

'So that's settled my future,' she said confidently. 'But I suppose we'll have to wait a while before we can be married.'

Julian swung round to face her. 'A darned long while,' he snapped, for now he was angry. 'What do you think I am? A cradle-snatcher?'

She smiled sweetly. 'But you've just proved you love me.' Naïvely she supposed his embrace signified he reciprocated her feelings and they would become engaged.

'My dear child, that wasn't love,' he told her brutally. 'At least, not the sort of love you deserve,' he amended, seeing the bewilderment in her face. 'You don't know anything about men, do you, little one? Nor do you understand your own feelings for what they are. Of course I'm very, very fond of you, but ...' He shook his head, wondering how to explain himself without hurting her.

'You mean what happened was just sex?' she asked slowly.

'Oh, lord, child!' He rumpled his hair. 'Don't you see, don't you understand you must learn something about life before you commit yourself? You've been shut up in that school like a convent . . .'

'Not the least like a convent,' she interrupted. 'The girls all have raves and crushes, some of them even have . . . experience. But I wasn't interested. I spent my holidays at Whiteladies and Aunt Linda asked young people to meet me, boys included. I despised them.' Her dark eyes became disdainful. 'They weren't like you, a stupid lot. I kept aloof from them, I was waiting for you to come back.'

'That was very foolish of you,' he said sternly, secretly dismayed.

She looked at him wistfully. 'You seemed to like kissing me,' she remarked ingenuously.

'Of course I did,' he almost shouted, 'but that's just it. God in heaven, Toni, I'd never forgive myself if I seduced you.'

'If you did you'd have to marry me,' she suggested hopefully.

He groaned. 'Delilah in embryo!'

'I don't think that's a very nice thing to say.'

'You're not behaving like a nice girl.'

'Who wants to be a nice girl?' she retorted, rising to her feet. 'I'd prefer to be desirable.'

She looked it, her dark eyes glowing, her slight body vibrant with sensuous allure.

Julian put his hands in front of his eyes.

'It's impossible, Toni,' he said quietly, 'I would be doing you a great wrong to marry you—tempting as the prospect is,' he smiled wryly. 'We wouldn't have a hope in hell of lasting happiness. All too soon you'd realise

39

you'd made a hideous mistake and find yourself chained to a middle-aged man. You've built up some sort of fantasy about me because I'm the only man you've known intimately, but my dear little girl, youth turns to youth, and I'm no chicken . . .'

He broke off, for Toni was not listening, she was watching him with a seductive smile, for all she had heard was the phrase, 'tempting as the prospect is'. She was sure that Julian wanted her as much as she wanted him and he was only trying to be sensible, seeing the matter as his parents would view it, but he would succumb in time, for what had reason to do with love? If only he would listen to the promptings of his heart, she thought, and forget about the gap in years which was so wholly unimportant,

Julian looked at her, looked away and said harshly:

'As a matter of fact I'm practically engaged to someone else.'

Jessamine Boycott had been rather more than the casual acquaintance Toni had surmised. She was a nice good-natured young woman and they had drawn together in their mutual exile. There had been nothing very exciting about their relationship, but he had decided that if he had to marry he might do a lot worse. She had come home at the same time as he had and he had promised to look her up.

Toni said nothing. In spite of the hot day she felt as if she had been plunged into an icy bath. When Julian ventured to glance at her, her face had become a white mask, her eyes black wells of anguish. Her senses were reeling under the heavy blow he had dealt them. He did not mean to be cruel, he had merely sought an effective means to put an end to her folly. He said lamely:

'I'm . . . I'm sorry.'

'You needn't be, it doesn't matter,' Toni returned, clutching at her pride. 'I'm glad you told me before I made a worse fool of myself.'

'It was a rather charming foolishness,' Julian sought to soften his rejection.

A little colour returned to her cheeks and her eyes gleamed.

'Don't be a hypocrite, you found it damned embarrassing,' she accused him. 'Let's forget it. I suppose she's quite a bit older than I?'

'Well, yes—she's twenty-six, I believe.'

'Old enough to understand her own feelings,' Toni said bitingly, reminding him of what he had said about herself. 'Will she expect me to be her bridesmaid?'

'We haven't got that far,' Julian replied, helpless before the wound he had inflicted. 'Toni . . .'

'Oh, let it be,' she cried impatiently. 'You had to tell me, and what time could be more auspicious than now when we're alone and talking so intimately?' She laughed a little wildly. 'Shall we go?'

She turned and began to walk back towards the car, and Julian followed her, cursing himself for his clumsy handling of an awkward situation, while she, quite aware of what he was thinking, derived a dreary satisfaction from his embarrassment.

The sheep were gathered round the car still hoping for largesse; they had to push their way through woolly backs to get to it. Toni wished she had some bread for them, feeling sympathetic towards them. They were not the only creatures on Long Mynd whose eager anticipations were unfulfilled.

41

CHAPTER THREE

THE sheep dispersed, Julian and Toni entered the car and he began to drive back the way they had come. The steep descent down the narrow twisty road required all his attention, and neither spoke. A car coming up necessitated moving over to the very edge of the crumbling verge to allow it to pass. Toni looked down into the depths below and almost wished the car would plunge downwards so that she and Julian might die together and thus defeat Miss Jessamine Boycott's hopes. Almost but not quite, for while she was alive there was still hope, and she was not yet defeated.

Since Julian's revelation she felt that she had aged by a decade, though it was only a few moments in time. From her mother she had inherited all the subtlety and guile of Latin women, who for centuries had had to wheedle all-powerful males to obtain what they wanted, nor were they over-scrupulous in their methods, being the race that had produced Lucretia Borgia and Catherine de Medici. Toni had no intention of allowing this unknown young woman to have a walkover, but she realised that her approach to Julian had been childish and crude. He had dismissed her overtures as fantasies of an emotional adolescent that would fade as she grew older. She had to make him understand that she had grown from a schoolgirl into a woman. Juliet, that fictional prototype of all passionate young females, was reputed to having been only fourteen, and she had been devoted enough to die for love. Toni was two years older and the same hot Italian blood ran in her veins. She knew that she had managed, to use the modern phrase, to turn Julian on in spite of his caution and restraint. He might declare that it was only sex, but he had desired her, and since he was also fond of her, it should not be impossible to turn that desire into something stronger, and since he would not see what was so obvious to her, that they were made for each other, she must be patient and find some means to make herself irresistible.

She recalled her success in *As You Like It* and the three youths, any one of whom she could have had by lifting a finger. Her attractions had been enhanced by the glamour of her stage performance. Julian had asked what she wanted to do and she would tell him she had made her choice. He probably would not approve, but he would be anxious to please her to atone for his rejection, and Mrs Thorne would help her with the practical details.

They reached the crossroads at the bottom of the hill, and Julian stopped the car, looking at her uncertainly. She was staring out of the windscreen apparently miles away from him, enjoying the vision she had conjured up of herself as a stage star and Julian at her feet.

'Would you like to go back to school?' he asked gently.

His voice dissipated her dream, and she turned her head towards him with a look of surprise.

'Good gracious, no!' she exclaimed. 'You promised to take me out to tea and we don't have to be back before dark.'

Julian seemed a little taken aback. 'But I thought ...' he began.

'That I'd want to slink away and nurse a broken heart?' She laughed with well feigned merriment. 'Hearts don't break that easily, you know. I played Rosalind, remember? "Men have died ... and worms have eaten them, but not for love." That applies to

43

women too.' Her eyes were brilliant in her pale face, sparkling with malice. 'We've got to decide what's to be done with me, haven't we? I can't stay at school after the end of the term.'

Julian looked at her uneasily. Could she so lightly dismiss the scene through which they had just passed? It would seem to confirm that her feelings had not been deeply hurt after all, which was exactly the impression Toni wanted to give him.

'Well, I thought we might run up Wenlock Edge and have tea at Much Wenlock. There's a nice little café there over an antique shop. That is ... er ... if you feel up to it?'

'Oh, I'm equal to anything,' she said with emphasis. 'Let's go.'

Church Stretton, on the outskirts of which Greystones was situated, lies between the two ridges of hills. The Long Mynd is on one side, Wenlock Edge on the other. The road rises up from the valley and runs along the rim of the Edge with, on a clear day, fine views on either side. Toni chatted gaily about their surroundings, acting the vivacious schoolgirl out for a treat. Julian must not be allowed to suspect the hard knot of pain and resentment at the core of her being. The bond that she had imagined bound them together did not exist. To her he was unique, saviour, protector, friend and lover rolled into one, but to him she was only a young cousin whom he had befriended and towards whom he had felt responsibility during her adolescence which he now considered was discharged.

They found the place Julian had suggested, an upstairs room above a shop in an old cottage, all oak beams and old-fashioned furniture. Over toasted home-made scones, Toni demanded:

44

'Tell me about this girl you're engaged to, what's she like?'

'I'm not engaged yet,' he corrected her hastily, and she noted the speed with which he made his disclaimer with glee. Was he already having second thoughts? He went on: 'There weren't many British girls out there and we seemed to get on well together. She's nice-looking, good-tempered and sympathetic. Jessamine Boycott is her name.' Toni recollected it from his letter, and she, poor fool, had dismissed his casual references as unimportant. 'Rather a pretty name, don't you think? She seemed to be a very sensible sort of young woman and she knows the country, so if I go out there again she wouldn't mind living there.'

Sensible, Toni thought scornfully—was that what a man wanted in a wife? To her passionate headstrong nature, Julian's description of his Jessamine sounded too tepid to be dangerous. She decided Julian had chosen Jessamine more because she was suitable than because he loved her. She said demurely:

'She sounds quite a paragon.'

Julian shot her a doubtful glance, suspecting sarcasm.

'She's not a prig.'

'Of course she couldn't be to appeal to you,' Toni said sweetly. 'And it must be a great advantage that she knows what horrors to expect if she has to live in Saudi Arabia.'

'Of course,' Julian returned curtly, not liking the mocking gleam in Toni's eyes, 'but the more immediate matter is your future, not mine.'

Toni turned her head away to stare out of the mul-lioned window. Until that afternoon she had believed that their futures were joined. For eight years she had adored him, but the very intimacy of their relationship

45

was against her. He regarded her as a member of the family and their brief moment of passion had shocked him. She sighed, wishing she had more experience to guide her, but she would learn, she was confident she had more to offer than any ordinary English girl.

'I would like to go on the stage,' she announced.

Miss Selby had told Julian that she had dramatic talent, but had dismissed an actress's career as undesirable, and Toni had never mentioned in any of her letters to him that she had any such aspirations. He said doubtfully:

'That's a profession where seventy per cent of its members are out of work.'

Toni smiled confidently. 'There's always room at the top.'

'Are you sure this isn't a passing phase? Your success as Rosalind has gone to your head a little, but it won't be like that. It's very hard work, with a great many disappointments, you should consider it very carefully.'

'Oh, I have,' Toni assured him mendaciously. 'My friend Annabel's mother knows all about it and she's been urging me to take up acting. It's the thing I do best.'

'But, my dear child, how will you set about it?'

Toni winced inwardly at the insistence upon that 'child.'

'I'm nearly grown up now, no longer a child,' she reproved him. At that moment she looked adult. 'I must go to R.A.D.A. It's the only training that's recognised by the profession. They won't take anyone who isn't promising, so if I fail the audition that will be that, but I shan't fail.'

Julian thought she was probably right. Not only did she possess striking looks and a low musical voice but force and temperament. He wished he had seen her Rosalind and said so.

'Oh no, Julian, you know you're bored stiff with Shakespeare,' Toni objected. She went on to tell him all Annabel and her mother had said, and the former's promise to use her influence. At the time she had paid little heed, for she believed Julian was her future. How incredibly naïve she had been, she thought sadly. As for her proposed career, she regarded it dispassionately, it was only a means to an end.

'We'll have to go into it all thoroughly,' Julian decided with a businesslike air, while he wondered if his mother would approve of Toni's choice of a profession, and whether the girl could be persuaded out of it if she did not. But as Toni had surmised, he was anxious to indulge her to counteract her obsession with himself.

'Certainly,' she agreed, though she knew he was completely ignorant of matters theatrical. Then as she had said once before, she added, 'I'm going to make you proud of me.'

'I'm that already,' he told her. 'You're quite beautiful, Toni.'

She looked at him enigmatically, tempted to inquire how she compared with Jessamine, but decided it were wiser to keep off the subject of the other girl, any reference to whom caused a black cloud of jealousy to descend upon her, threatening her self-control. She was instinctively aware that any emotional display would only antagonise Julian, so she must continue to 'play it cool.'

But underneath her surface calm was a misery as yet unplumbed. That would be for the concealing dark when he had left her and she faced her desolation during the long night hours—Julian contemplating a wife and children in a home where she would have no place.

47

Yearningly she studied his straight features and lean lithe figure, avoiding meeting the bright blue eyes that might discern too much. Julian, her Julian was here at last, but he had come to tell her that he was about to put an insurmountable barrier between them.

For all that he seemed to be in no hurry to part with her. After tea he drove her around the countryside, stopping here and there to admire a particularly fine view, while he gave her intimate details concerning the people he had met and his life abroad, but he did not mention Jessamine again, and neither did she. Since she would miss her supper, they had a meal at a roadside café, so that by the time they returned to Greystones the sun had set and the long northern twilight lay over the land. The curtains were drawn when they reached the front of the house, and a light showed above the fanlight of the front door, there was no one in sight. Julian said he would not come in as he had had enough of Miss Selby for one day, and as they stood together in the drive, Toni's control slipped.

'Thank you for a lovely afternoon,' she murmured, and flinging her arms about his neck she clung to him. He kissed her gently on the cheek, then something of her urgency spreading to him, again not so gently upon her mouth. The front door opened, releasing a flood of light, and the matron's reproving voice reached them.

'Antonia, is that you? You're very late.'

Gently Julian disengaged himself and moved towards the woman, apologising for keeping Toni so long. It had been such a beautiful evening and they had so much to talk about, but Toni sensed he hardly knew what he was saying.

'Goodnight, cousin Julian,' she called for the matron's benefit, as she passed into the hall, her eyes alight with triumph.

48

Julian drove away assuring himself that she was still only a child and did not know what she was doing.

But Toni knew very well, and Julian's embrace had elated her. Given time and opportunity she believed she could combat Miss Jessamine Boycott and all her suitability. Unfortunately she had little time and would have to make her opportunities.

Toni was auditioned and enrolled for the autumn term at R.A.D.A. amid dire mutterings of waiting lists and overcrowding. Mrs Thorne had been her advocate and pulled strings shamelessly. Annabel told Toni:

'Poor Ma still hankers after the stage. She hoped that I'd follow in her footsteps, but I've not inherited her talent. She'll be glad to push you in my stead, and you're lucky. She's lots of influence.'

'You won't mind?' Toni asked diffidently.

'Good gracious, no, I'll be glad to get her off my back so I can do what I want to without feeling guilty.' Annabel was interested in speech therapy. 'Go on and set the Thames alight. I'm sure you can do it, you've got everything.'

Everything but the one thing that Toni wanted most.

Julian had persuaded his parents to agree to Toni's choice of a profession, though they did not like it. Linda admitted that it was difficult to decide what the girl was suited for, and she did not want the responsibility for her at Whiteladies. When Mrs Thorne suggested Toni should live with her and she would look after her, she accepted the arrangement with relief.

Julian had three months' leave after his long spell of duty, which he was to spend at home to please his parents. Toni also was back at Whiteladies for her summer holidays before she went to London. Inevitably they were thrown together, since the Everards' wide circle of acquaintances invited them both to all the local functions. August teemed with gymkhanas, flower shows, cricket matches and tennis tournaments. For the last both were in demand, for they were exceptional players, and they rode in the jumping contests at local shows. Polly the pony had been retired and Toni now possessed a thoroughbred mare.

But Julian held aloof from her as much as possible; their old affectionate intimacy had gone for ever. Toni divined his reason; he meant to marry his Jessamine and install her at Whiteladies, so he wished to avoid any complications with herself. Though his changed attitude wounded her, Toni guessed its cause and that afforded her some satisfaction. If only she were older and more experienced, she thought regretfully, she could break down the barrier between them and scotch Miss Boycott's aspirations, for Julian did not seem to be a very ardent lover. Though the lady must have reached England, he had not gone to see her. But Toni feared that any move upon her own part would further antagonise Julian. He was determined not to have an affair with a teenager on his own doorstep.

Though she schooled herself to accept his neglect, Toni did not find it easy to restrain her passionate nature, and when after a couple of uneasy weeks she discovered that Jessamine Boycott had actually been asked to stay, jealousy was added to her torment. Unwise though it might be, she resolved to make one last appeal to Julian before the other girl arrived on the scene.

She waylaid him on his return from a fishing expedition, waiting while he garaged his car. The setting sun gilded the garden, throwing long shadows over the velvety lawns. Whiteladies possessed extensive grounds; the house itself was half-timbered and festooned with climbing roses. It had been built on the remains of a Carmelite convent, hence its name, and it was supposed to be haunted by a white nun who had broken her vows for love and paid the penalty, though none of the family had ever seen her. Toni had changed for the evening into a long white dress, with a lacy shawl over her head and shoulders, so that she might have been the wraith herself.

As Julian emerged from the garage, she said: 'I want to talk to you.'

'Do you, my dear?' He barely glanced at her. 'But isn't it nearly dinner time? I have to change, you know.'

A subterfuge; dinner was nearly an hour away.

'I won't keep you long. Come down to the rose garden. The roses are so beautiful and I don't believe you ever look at them.'

He came unwillingly. The rose garden was below the lawns, concealed from the house by a high brick wall that enclosed it. It was paved between the beds and in the centre was a small pond in which goldfish swam among lily pads. Edgar Everard spent all his spare time tending it. He loved his roses, but he was attending a parochial meeting that evening, as Toni knew.

'I do come here quite often with Dad,' Julian told her, as they passed through the wrought iron gate that gave access to it. 'Your Uncle makes sure of that, he's so proud of his blooms.'

He avoided looking at her, for in her flowing dress, close-fitting about her body but flaring out into soft folds round her feet, the flimsy shawl softening but not obscuring her sculptured neck and shoulders and her shadowy hair, Toni looked seductive. The only touch of colour about her were her red lips and the dark red rose she had gathered earlier and pinned in the front of her bodice.

She dismissed Edgar Everard and his roses with a wave of one slim hand. 'Julian, what has gone wrong? You act like a stranger towards me and we used to be such pals.'

Imperceptibly he drew further away from her.

'You were a child,' he reminded her. 'I can't continue to treat you like a kid now you're a young woman.'

'So you admit I'm grown up?'

'Hardly that ... yet.'

'But that's no reason why you should regard me as a leper,' she cried vehemently. Her eyes gleamed suddenly; 'Unless you're afraid?'

'Perhaps I am,' he admitted, drawing a pattern with the toe of his shoe on the paving stones. Then he threw back his head and looked at her, his eyes glittering with blue fire.

'You've become a woman, my darling, and a damned attractive one, but I must reiterate how disastrous a union between us would be. I'm years too old for you, you've all your life in front of you with success, perhaps even fame just round the corner, for Mrs Thorne has persuaded us all you've a unique talent. My life is half over, the best years gone. I'd be a heel to take advantage of your youthful affection for me. You must give your heart to a younger man who'll make you forget me ...'

'No one could ever do that,' she broke in, her voice quivering with emotion. 'Don't you know you're everything to me, Julian? I don't care how old you are, age has nothing to do with it. When you go away the sun drops out of my sky and I merely exist until you come again to bring me to life. I can't help being young, but that will remedy with time. We'll grow closer as I become older and you're still in your prime. You needn't even marry me, only love me a little.'

Her great eyes glowed with passion and she clutched

his arm with shaking fingers. She felt his muscles become rigid under her clasp and he went very white under his tan. Then with an effort he relaxed, slipping his arm around her and leading her to a wooden seat overlooking the pool. He sat down and drew her down beside him.

'Toni darling, don't talk like that,' he besought her. 'You don't know what you're saying. Of course I'll always love you, and it's because I think so much of you I want you to be happy. This ... this thing you have for me is only an infatuation, a fixation. It'll fade when you enter the adult world and win the admiration you deserve. What about that wonderful career you're about to embark upon?'

'Oh, that ... I don't know if I'm going to have a career, it's just something to do ... to make you notice me.'

'Oh, Toni, what a baby you are!' He laughed a little forcedly. 'As if I wasn't always aware of you ...' He stopped afraid he had said too much. Toni's head was on his shoulder, her hair soft against his cheek, her shawl having slipped to the ground. She snuggled closer within his encircling arm and said dreamily:

'This is how you used to hold me when I was a frightened child. Everything had gone and there was only you. There's still only you.'

She raised her head and kissed his bronzed cheek. To her dismay he pushed her aside and sprang to his feet.

'Good God, girl, don't do that! I'm only human.'

'But I want you to be human.'

She came to him then, twining her arms about his neck, and the dam broke. All the passionate fervour of her nature rose in response to his fierce kisses, their bodies seemed to fuse and she knew an ecstasy that was pain. Spent, she lay back in his arms at length, her eyes

53

alight with triumph—a triumph that was shortlived.

Gently Julian put her away from him, allowing her to subside upon the seat. He stood before her, his face hardening as he regained his self-control, while her own racing pulses began to slow. When at length he spoke his voice was cold and clipped.

'I'm sorry about that, Toni, but I thought you understood on Long Mynd how I felt. You're innocent, I know, but there are some things you should learn before you go out into the world for your own protection, things I don't suppose you were taught at school.' He smiled faintly, recalling Miss Selby's starched virginity. 'Not all men are as scrupulous as I, and if given such open invitation, they'll misinterpret your actions. I'd hate some swine to take advantage of you.'

Toni sighed with exasperation. No man would ever be anything to her except himself, but she was vexed with herself for her lack of self-control, which had given him an excuse to lecture her.

'You think I'm a forward minx?' she asked.

'I wouldn't say that. Merely a little too impetuous.'

'Very nicely put,' she gibed. She looked down at her hands clasped in her lap and shivered. 'Would you give me my shawl, please?'

It lay between them, a white heap on the paving. Julian picked it up, the flimsy stuff looking frail in his strong hands. Hands that have torn my heart in twain, Toni thought dramatically. The extravagant phrase pleased her, but it was the only childish thing about her. Her eyes veiled by her long lashes held all the suffering of a grown woman.

Julian laid the shawl across her shoulders, careful not to touch her. She noticed that.

'Are you so inflammable?' she asked scornfully.

He smiled wryly. 'I'm afraid so. Most men are where

beautiful women are concerned. It's something you'll have to learn to cope with.'

'I'll do that.' She would permit no liberties from other men. The knowledge that she could so affect Julian gave her a sense of dreary triumph, but it was no victory if he despised himself for yielding to her. He felt he was being unfaithful to Jessamine, and that was precisely what she had tried to do, make him forget the other woman. With deliberate malice she said carelessly:

'I suppose your Jessamine is too well brought up to tempt you with impetuous impulses.'

'She's more reserved than you are,' he returned evasively.

'Meaning that she doesn't throw herself at your head like I do?'

'Oh please, Toni, let it be,' he said despairingly. 'You know I didn't mean that. But she's older ...'

'Of course, age is everything, isn't it? You can still excuse me on the plea of being an emotional adolescent. But I won't always be one, you know, and then ...'

She paused, not sure whether to utter a warning or a threat.

'By then you'll have so many handsome adorers you'll have forgotten all about an old has-been like me,' he said cheerfully, with a curiously wistful expression in his eyes.

Toni stood up, shaking out her skirts. The rose pinned to the front of her dress was, she noticed, crushed and drooping. She unpinned it, saying imperiously:

'Please pick me another one, Julian, since you've done for this one with your violence.'

He flushed at her tone, as she noticed with pleasure, but he obediently turned to the rose beds to seek a crimson bloom. Her eyes dwelt longingly on the rough gold of his hair, gilded by the last rays of the setting sun, but it would have given her great pleasure to stick a knife into him. He persisted in misunderstanding her because he did not want her woman's love, he had only cared for her when she was an undemanding child. She was of mixed blood, her maternal ancestry unknown, too exotic and unpredictable to be a satisfactory wife, so he resented her because she had shaken his allegiance to the impeccable Jessamine Boycott who was probably too coldblooded to seek to arouse his ardour. Her instinct told her he was making the wrong choice. Together they could have created the 'many-splendoured thing', compounded not only of passion but of intimacy shared and affinity, for they would have been friends before they were lovers, but no, he preferred his English blonde who would never raise him to heights of rapture, she thought bitterly, as he handed her a red rose. Mechanically she fastened it to her dress while he watched her, fully aware of why he did not offer to do it for her. But he had no need to fear further advances, she would not offend again.

She said coolly: 'I've been very foolish. Being a besotted teenager, I've never seen you as you really are. Because you rescued me out in Italy I put you on a pedestal, making a romantic figure out of you, a sort of knight in armour—schoolgirls do get these idiotic crushes. But tonight you've opened my eyes. As you said, you're very human and rather weak. I'll be no further embarrassment to you.'

He hesitated, on the verge of a protest. Toni watched him with bright glittering eyes, sensing that he did not altogether enjoy being toppled from his pedestal, and no man likes to be called weak. But he thought better of it, and said formally;

'Believe me, Toni, I only want what is best for you. I

shall always have your welfare at heart.'

'And of course you know what's best for me?'

'I'm sure of it.'

'You always do the right thing, don't you?' she told him mockingly. 'But I'm not sure it wouldn't have been kinder to have left me in Italy, where I belonged.'

She swept past him out of the wrought iron gate without giving him time to respond to her exaggerated exit line. She did not see him stoop and pick up the faded rose she had discarded.

That night Toni talked and laughed over dinner with an almost hectic gaiety, so that her aunt and uncle were astonished. She was coming to life at last, and how beautiful she looked when she was animated. But Julian was morose and silent, watching her with a glitter in his eyes. Good, she thought; he didn't like what I said to him in the rose garden, he resents his great rescue act being questioned. But it had been partly true, she never had felt she really belonged at Whiteladies, only Julian could have made her part of it and he had failed her.

When the meal was ended, Julian suggested to his father that they should go down to the local pub.

'An indulgence I'll have to forgo when Jessamine arrives,' he said with a grin.

'If I know modern girls she'll want to come too,' Edgar remarked, but he accepted his son's invitation with alacrity.

When they had gone, Toni excused herself and went to her room. There she gave way to her frustration and despair with floods of tears. It was a long time before she was calm enough to sleep.

CHAPTER FOUR

JULIAN's request that Jessamine Boycott be asked to stay
had filled Linda with delight. It could only mean that
her son was at last serious about a girl. As both of the
men of the family were out all day helping with the
harvesting, Toni became the unwilling recipient of her
speculations. Though the girl tried to school herself to
a show of indifference she could not wholly conceal her
chagrin. Linda ascribed her lack of enthusiasm to a
little natural pique and told her kindly:

'Perhaps you feel your nose has been put out of
joint, as Julian was so devoted to you when you were a
child, but it's only natural he should turn to a woman
nearer his age, and you've an exciting new life ahead of
you, so you mustn't grudge him his happiness.'

Words that were bitter gall to Toni. She returned: 'I
don't grudge him anything that will make him happy.'
Which she did not believe Jessamine could do.

'I'm sure this girl will if she's the right sort, as we
shall soon see. Julian needs a wife and he's becoming
more interested in the work on the estate. Edgar says
he's been driving the combine. You know, Toni, your
uncle's beginning to feel his age, and if Julian isn't
prepared to take over we'll have to sell out. Of course
we don't want to press him, we've always insisted he'd a
right to live his own life, but a family might cure his
wanderlust. He always talks about retiring here eventually, but time's running out.'

'But what would you do?' Toni asked, unable to
visualise Linda anywhere except presiding over Whiteladies.

'Oh, your uncle and I will move into a cottage on the

estate and leave the young people in possession. A lot depends upon whether this girl likes the house.'

'She'll be hard to please if she doesn't.' Toni looked appreciatively round the room in which they were sitting. She realised with a pang that if Julian brought home a bride there would be no place for her there any longer. Although she had never fitted into the frame of the Everards' social environment she was attached to the old house.

'She lives in London so she mayn't like the country,' Linda observed, 'or she may want something more modern. At least your future is settled, since you've decided to go on the stage.'

'That must be a great relief to you,' Toni said with a touch of bitterness. 'I'd hate to become an embarrassment to you.'

'Oh, my dear, you'd never be that,' Linda cried insincerely, for that was exactly what she feared Toni's presence at Whiteladies might become. She was confident that if Julian married and started a family his wife would be an advocate for a permanent home. Foreign assignments were all very well for a single man, but women were all for settling down. It was very necessary that Toni should strike out on her own.

Toni knew exactly what she was thinking, her life seemed to be disintegrating. Julian's affection had been dissolved by the discovery that she was no longer a child he could pet and indulge, and was liable to awkward reactions, and now the security of her home was threatened. At that moment she felt very lost and young, her self-confidence ebbing. Suppose she failed to make good in spite of Mrs Thorne's assurances? What would become of her?

On the day that Jessamine was expected, Julian left early to meet her in Shrewsbury, whence she was coming by train. She was not due until the afternoon, but he said he had some business to transact in the town and they would be back in time for dinner. Linda was in quite a flutter. They didn't often have visitors actually staying in the house and she was anxious to make a good impression. She had a long session with Mrs Craddock about the menu and the arrangements for the evening, then she called to Toni to lend her a hand with making the visitor's bed. Toni went unwillingly; she was becoming heartily tired of the subject of Miss Jessamine Boycott before she had even arrived.

The guest room was situated in front of the house and having been recently redecorated showed no signs of the shabbiness that was beginning to invade some parts of it. Toni had long since ceased to occupy the dressing room next to Julian. Her room, looking over the lands at the back, was the fourth bedroom on the first floor.

Together she and Linda made up the wide bed with lavender-scented linen sheets and cellular blankets. Over their task, Mrs Everard continued to enthuse about the advent of Jessamine and her hopes and fears, blind to Toni's discomfort. To distract her, Toni asked if Julian had ever shown interest in any other girl. He had been twenty-five when she had met him, old enough to have had some amorous adventures. Linda admitted that there had been someone when he was very young, who had spent a weekend with them.

'A divorced actress's daughter,' she told her, 'a dreadful flashy-looking creature. I'm thankful to say the affair fizzled out. Thank goodness Jessamine seems to be a steady sort of girl, and she's very well connected.'

Toni felt a moment's chill. Could she herself be described as flashy? And her maternal connections were not exactly aristocratic—Maria had been a peasant girl. But surely such considerations were not really important—if one loved. She said a little maliciously:

'I understand Miss Boycott is ready to return to Saudi Arabia with Julian if he's sent out there again.'

Linda smiled wisely. 'She says so now, no doubt, but she'll change her tune when they're married, especially when there's a baby on the way.'

Toni's colour ebbed. That was something she had not considered. Children would place Julian far beyond her reach, for she knew he would be a most devoted father.

'What's the matter?' her aunt asked, noting her pallor.

'It ... it's so hot today,' Toni murmured.

'No more than it has been lately. For goodness' sake, Toni, don't go and be ill just when this girl's coming.'

'I'm all right.' Toni began feverishly to tuck in the bedclothes. 'It's to be hoped Miss Boycott comes up to your expectations.'

'Oh, I'm sure she will,' Linda declared. 'Julian's old enough now to pick someone suitable, and she sounds thoroughly nice.'

Toni recalled that Julian had cast some doubts upon her own claim to niceness. She did not think it was a necessary adjunct towards winning a man's love.

'*Is* he in love with her?' she asked doubtfully.

'He wouldn't want to marry her if he wasn't,' Linda declared. 'Of course he's past the age of blind infatuation and capable of using some discrimination. I don't think I'll be disappointed in his choice.'

It needed all Toni's self-control to complete her task, drawing the silk coverlet over the bed which she would like to have strewn with thistles. Linda's smug complacency stung her unbearably. She could imagine her consternation if Julian wanted to marry herself.

61

Apart from her extreme youth, that damnable lack of years that baulked her, Linda would consider she was too intense and temperamental to be a satisfactory wife for her son. Toni was under no illusions regarding her aunt's opinion of her, and she had already shown she was a misfit in the Everards' conventional circle. Writhing inwardly, Toni thought wryly that R.A.D.A. would not have to teach her much about acting. She was playing a part all the time. Her natural inclination was to put arsenic in Jessamine Boycott's after-dinner coffee, but her rival would have no such vicious urges; she was too English and too nice. Toni gave the pillows a savage thump.

'What did you do that for?' Linda asked, smoothing them out. She looked at her great-niece anxiously. 'I do hope you'll be pleasant to Jessamine. It's most important we should all make her feel welcome for Julian's sake.'

'I'll try to behave like a lady,' Toni promised with an ironic lift of her brows.

'You should have learned that at your expensive school,' Linda told her tartly. 'We couldn't have afforded it if Julian hadn't helped, but he was determined you should have the best, so mind you do him credit. He's also offered to assist with your drama course fees. Of course he can't do anything more for you if he marries.'

'I don't want him to,' Toni cried, humiliated by this revelation. Julian was ready to help with her fees to get her out of his way. She had known about the school, that was different. She had assumed that Julian naturally wanted her to be well educated to be a fit companion for him in their life together. 'I hope to earn my living when I leave the Academy,' she went on. 'If I'm a success I might repay something. As it is it seems like with the Chinese, when Julian saved my life he had to assume responsibility for me ever after.'

'Don't exaggerate so,' Linda said severely. 'Of course we all wanted to do our best for poor Lewis's daughter.'

'Then if I weren't his child you wouldn't have done anything?'

'If you weren't you wouldn't be here. I don't know what you're talking about, Toni, all I ask is that you make yourself amiable to Jessamine.'

'I'll do my best,' Toni agreed reluctantly. Her great-aunt had no idea what an ordeal she had to face. She added flippantly: 'I suppose Julian's had lots of affairs he hasn't told you about?'

'Oh really, child, what things you say! Of course he doesn't confide in me about that sort of thing, but being a normal man and at his age ...' She broke off. 'It's not a fit subject for an innocent girl like you.'

Toni laughed. 'Not all that innocent, Zia Linda. This is a permissive age and no one thinks innocence worth preserving.'

As she had hoped, Linda looked shocked. Her aunt's emphasis upon her unsophistication had needled her.

'Toni, you're not implying ...?'

Toni laughed again. 'Don't worry, Zia, I'm not that way inclined. I'm only interested in my ... profession.'

'Young people nowadays are so regrettably free in their speech,' Linda said repressively as they left the bedroom.

As expected Jessamine arrived in time for dinner, to serve which Mrs Craddock had agreed to stay late so that Linda would be free. Toni heard the voices in the hall while she was changing, for the Everards always dressed for dinner, Mrs Everard's raised in greeting, Julian and his father's deeper tones and a light affected articulation which must be Jessamine's. She had de-

63

liberately left her door slightly ajar and as they came upstairs she heard the visitor say:

'It's absolutely gorgeous! I love old houses, such atmosphere. Ju darling, you're awfully lucky to live in such a place.'

Toni winced at the abbreviation. Never before had anyone called Julian 'Ju', and it sounded horrible. Jessamine was seeking to ingratiate herself by praising the house. Toni admitted it was a more subtle approach than her own of incredible naïveté. She wondered if it were genuine.

A mood of defiance took possession of her. Linda expected her to efface herself, Julian would treat her with indifference, and the girl with the affected voice, who was assessing his home with the idea of living there, had no doubt been told little Toni was only a negligible schoolgirl.

But Antonia Luisa Everard was not going to allow herself to be overlooked. Nature at least had been kind to her by endowing her with unusual looks. She would make Julian notice her.

She searched through her wardrobe and found a flaming chiffon dress which she had bought unknown to Linda with Edgar's generous Christmas cheque. It was a protest against the sober garments Linda insisted upon choosing for her. Instinctively she knew how striking she would appear in it. Tonight she would give it an airing. She selected a pair of barbaric gold ear-rings Annabel had given her, saying they would suit her, and a necklace of garnets set in gold for her neck. The costume accentuated her Italian beauty. She looked like Carmen, she thought, surveying herself in the mirror, and hummed the tune of the *Habañera*. 'If I love thee, then beware!'

She waited to go downstairs until she knew they

would be assembled in Linda's drawing room for pre-dinner apéritifs. As she entered the room she saw Jessamine at once. She was sitting in the chair that Julian had occupied when Toni was first introduced to her great-aunt. She recalled that moment with a stab—how she had clung to Julian and how sweet he had been to her. The beams from the setting sun coming in through the open windows filled the room with a golden glow, gilding Jessamine's blonde hair, as it also did Julian's as he stood behind her chair. He looked incredibly youthful, his brown face still unlined except for the sun wrinkles about his eyes. He was slim as a boy in the dinner jacket he had put on in Jessamine's honour. Jessamine herself was the type described as an English rose, fresh-complexioned, a little on the plump side, with large blue eyes, not vivid blue like Julian's but tinged with grey. She had to tint her brows and lashes, which were by nature sandy. She wore a trouser suit in blue with a high-necked mandarin tunic. Toni with her black hair and eyes, matt white skin and flaming drapery looked like an exotic flower among all the Everards and Jessamine's fairness.

Julian took in Toni's appearance in one swift glance as she came towards them and his brow contracted in a frown, but his voice betrayed no disapproval as he stepped forward to introduce her.

'This is my little cousin Toni, Jess. She's going to be an actress, hence the ... er ... flamboyance.'

Toni smiled serenely. She had expected him to dislike her flaming dress, which made her like a poppy among corn, but that had been her intention. She had hoped to make an impression and judging by Jessamine's slightly surprised look she had succeeded. She nodded towards the older girl, who had remained seated, and said politely:

'How are you? I hope you had a pleasant journey.'

'Not too bad,' Jessamine returned. 'Had to change at Hereford which was a bit of a bore, but luckily the train was nearly on time, so Ju didn't have long to wait.'

She was assessing Toni critically; she had not been prepared for such looks, nor the contralto slightly sexy voice. From Julian's description of his cousin and her tragic history, she had expected a small shrinking creature who would be grateful for any kindness shown to her, and she had been prepared to be kind to the poor little thing, since Julian seemed to be fond of her. This girl had poise and self-possession, and looked adult. She would resent kindness as patronage and would possibly be impudent. Instinctively Jessamine sensed a rival.

'Sherry, Toni?' Julian asked, and went to pour one for her.

Jessamine raised arched painted eyebrows, inquiring: 'Does she drink?'

'Of course,' Toni answered her. 'Youth today is precocious, didn't you know that?'

'More's the pity,' Jessamine declared.

'Why so?' Toni queried blandly.

'Because if teenagers experience everything too young they have nothing to enjoy in later life,' Jessamine explained. 'I had my first glass of wine on my twenty-first birthday, and it was an event worth waiting for.'

Toni took the wine glass from Julian, smiling mischievously. 'I bet it was,' she agreed, 'but you see in Italy even babies drink red wine.'

She sat down on a low stool, her flimsy skirts billowing round her. From the low-cut bodice her dark head rose proudly on its long graceful neck.

A most unsuitable ensemble for a teenager, Jessamine thought; the girl was evidently spoiled and needed putting in her place. She said acidly: 'Ah yes, I was forgetting—you're Italian, aren't you?' She made it sound as if it were something disreputable.

'Only half, the other half is English,' Toni pointed out. 'I'm an Everard, though I mayn't look like one.'

She lifted her white chin defiantly. It was the one sure thing she had to cling to, the reason why she was there.

'But you take after your mother?'

'In colouring, yes.'

'Latin women are often beautiful as girls, but they coarsen and put on weight quite early,' Jessamine remarked cattily. She was not normally a cat, but Toni's appearance had disconcerted her; she had an uneasy feeling that Julian could not live in close proximity to so much beauty and remain indifferent to it. She noticed how often his eyes strayed towards the brilliant figure on the stool.

'Do they now?' Toni smiled serenely, divining what was causing the other girl to be spiteful. 'But as I said I'm only half Latin, Miss Boycott, and I'm too energetic to put on weight. I'm grateful to my Italian blood for giving me temperament.'

'Toni gave a wonderful performance in the school play,' Linda intervened, put out by the apparent antipathy between the two girls. Toni had promised to behave and she had said nothing outrageous as yet, but that dress!—She wished she had inquired what her niece intended to wear. She had no idea she possessed such a garment.

'The standard isn't usually very high in school drama,' Jessamine drawled. 'But I wish you every success, Toni.'

That was sincere, for success would keep Toni away from Whiteladies and break her association with Julian.

'Thank you, Miss Boycott.'

'Oh, please call me Jess, everyone does,' Jessamine requested. Toni's Miss Boycott made her feel about forty.

'Yes, do,' Julian told her. 'She's not another aunt, you know.'

'Only my prospective cousin,' Toni purred, flashing him a provocative glance, and saw him bite his lip. So he had not made up his mind yet.

Then Mrs Craddock appeared to tell them the meal was served and they all moved towards the dining room, Julian gallantly arming his guest.

The dining room at Whiteladies was another long low room, with a panelled wainscot half way up its walls. As it was growing dark the table was lit by candles in three-branched candelabra, but the curtains were undrawn to show a sky in which daylight still lingered and later would be lit by the moon. Several portraits of departed Everards hung on the walls with the same keen blue eyes that had been reproduced in Edgar and Julian. Mr and Mrs Everard sat at the head and foot of the table with Julian and Jessamine on one side and Toni opposite to them. The food was simple and good, fresh trout that Julian had caught for a starter, followed by chicken, a bird from the farm, and then raspberries in thick frozen cream from the same source. It was all a little stately and old-fashioned, but Jessamine rhapsodied over everything, the room, the food, the candlelight, so restful, unlike the glare of electricity, but Toni detected a certain shrewdness in her many questions. She was probing to discover if the farm paid and what were its prospects. Then she said:

'I wonder, Ju, how you can bear to tear yourself away from all this to take positions abroad.'

'When I was a boy rural life didn't appeal to me—

well, not as a fixture. Whiteladies is splendid for holidays, but it's a bit of a backwater.'

'You find more life in the oil territories?'

He grinned. 'I'm all for new experiences.'

Jessamine switched to their life in Saudi Arabia; her conversation punctuated with 'Ju, do you remember so and so?'

Toni listened in silence with a little enigmatical smile curving her well shaped mouth, for Julian's glance was upon her more and more frequently as if he could not keep his eyes away from her. The candlelight which was kind to Jessamine was even more so to her, making her eyes appear dark wells of mystery. The seating arrangement permitted him to watch her across the table, while apparently absorbed in his conversation with Jessamine. Toni had, as she had hoped to do, put the older girl in the shade; compared with her Jessamine looked colourless and insipid, and Julian was aware of it. That was why he had looked so disapproving when Toni had appeared, deeming it ill manners for a chit of a schoolgirl to dress to eclipse a guest, but he was dazzled by the result. Jessamine was trying to exclude her by referring to that period in his life in which she had no part. Toni recognised her tactics and did not resent them. She did not blame Jessamine for using every weapon she could, as she intended to do the same herself.

Saudi Arabia exhausted as a topic, talk reverted to the house. Jessamine asked if there was a ghost.

'Surely there must be,' she declared. 'Presumably one of a nun, since it's built on a convent site.' She looked around the table eagerly.

'You're quite right,' Linda told her. 'There is supposed to be one, a white nun, but none of us have ever seen her. We can't be sensitive enough.'

'Antonia looks as if she might be,' Jessamine suggested. Blue eyes met black across the table. Jessamine managing to convey that such sensitivity was idiocy.

'I haven't had the pleasure of meeting her yet,' Toni returned calmly.

'Ooh! It would hardly be a pleasure, would it? Interesting perhaps, but what's the story?'

'The usual one,' Julian told her. 'Broken vows, unpleasant immolation, predictable haunting. The back wall of the kitchen incorporates some of the old convent precincts. Tradition says that's where she was walled up.'

'I never knew that,' Toni was surprised. 'Although I've lived here for so long.'

'We kept it from you,' Linda explained, 'we thought you were too nervous and impressionable.'

'There, what did I tell you?' Jessamine cried triumphantly. 'She's just the sort to imagine ghosts. But I'm not nervous and I'd like to see the place, but preferably by daylight.'

'There's nothing much to see,' said Julian. 'Only a blank wall with a bricked-in archway which lent itself to the supposition, probably quite erroneously.'

'Don't spoil it,' Jessamine besought him. 'Why shouldn't it be the place?' She pensively peeled a peach. 'Personally I think the woman must have been a bit of a fool. She must have known what a gruesome penalty she was risking.'

'If she really loved she'd chance it,' Toni cried vehemently. 'She wouldn't be able to help herself.'

Her eyes glowed and as they met Julian's kindled a flickering flame in his. Instantly he looked down at the table, Toni turned her head away and Jessamine said scornfully:

'What a very Latin point of view!'

'Toni's very young and romantic,' Julian observed. 'She believes all is well worth losing for love.'

Toni thought furiously, I'll make you believe it too one day!

Linda rose and suggested that they adjourned for coffee in the drawing room; the faithful daily was staying to clear and wash up, but she asked Toni to come with her to fetch the coffee.

'Can't I help?' Jessamine asked, eager to ingratiate herself.

'Oh no, dear, we'll manage. You go and entertain Julian,' Linda insisted. In the kitchen she remarked:

'She's just the sort of girl I hoped Julian would take .up with.'

Unable to restrain herself, Toni snapped:

'She'd bore me to death if I had to live with her!'

'Then it's a good thing it's not you who is going to do that,' Linda said reprovingly. 'Those placid types are much more restful than temperamental ones. Remember that, my dear, husbands don't appreciate fireworks.'

'Oh, I'm never going to marry,' Toni declared as she picked up the tray of coffee cups. If she could not have Julian, she vowed, she would remain a spinster all her life.

The moon had risen and was pouring silver light over the gardens surrounding Whiteladies. It was a mild summer night and when they had finished their coffee Julian asked Jessamine if she were too tired to take a stroll outside.

'It seems too lovely to stay indoors,' he said, drawing back the curtains and peering through the window. 'I can almost smell the scent of roses from here.

Jessamine rose with alacrity. 'Shall I need a coat?'

'I hardly think so.'

'I'll just get a stole,' she decided. 'After being in a hot country one has to be careful not to get a chill.'

'Toni'll fetch it for you,' Linda suggested.

'Oh, I wouldn't dream of troubling her,' Jessamine said hurriedly, and ran out of the room.

Toni went to the window and leaned her head against the frame. On many such a night she and Julian had gone out together searching for badgers in the woods, listening to the owls or, earlier in the year, the nightingale. Sometimes they had saddled his horse and her pony and gone for a ride. Both were attracted by the mysteries of the night and the unearthly radiance of the moon. But those days of happy companionship were gone for ever. He had brought this blonde usurper into their lives and was waiting to canoodle with her in the rose garden. She became aware that he was standing close behind her, and turned her head to look at him, divining that he too was remembering their expeditions.

'Too bad we have to grow up,' he said.

'But you always were grown up,' she pointed out.

'But I was able to relive my boyhood with you, show you all my youthful haunts.' He sighed. 'You'll have to find another playmate, Toni.'

'I'm grown up too now,' she returned, and flinched from his mocking smile. 'There'll be no more playtime,' she added, and turned away as Jessamine came back into the room wearing a white shawl over her shoulders.

Julian went to meet her, drawing her arm possessively though his. They went out together and Toni watched them, enveloped in a fierce cloud of jealousy.

'Well, since they've gone out, we might as well turn on the television,' Edgar announced, and ambled over to the set. Linda took out her knitting; she was always making something, socks, sweaters or scarves—she liked to keep her fingers employed while she watched. The calm domesticity of the scene rasped on Toni's nerves, and she felt too restless to sit down. Mind and heart were occupied with the pair in the garden. What were they doing, what were they saying? With anguish she pictured Jessamine in Julian's arms. Was that insipid creature capable of experiencing the fierce ecstasy that had thrilled herself when he had embraced her? She could not imagine it, and she hoped that Jessamine was frigid. But Julian was not an inexperienced boy, he would know how to rouse her, and would have no scruples about doing so since she was the right age to receive his lovemaking.

Finally Toni left the room with a murmured excuse. Taking a dark cloak off a peg in the hall, one belonging to Linda, she went out of doors. The silver splendour of the moon threw inky shadows across the pools of argent. She went round to the back of the house, and found the bricked-up archway Julian had mentioned. She had noticed it before but had not known its significance. Had Linda really believed the story would frighten her? There had been many more formidable things at Whiteladies to face than a poor little ghost. Jessamine, she decided, would never run the hazard of a nasty death for the love of any man, even Julian. She was too sensible. She herself would perform any rash action that would win for her her heart's desire. So she had indicated at dinner, and Julian had said she was young and romantic. Did one forget how to feel as one grew older? She hoped the poor nun had known some hours of bliss before she was caught and sentenced. The story did not say what had happened to her lover. Had he been executed too in a more conventional way, or had he escaped congratulating himself it was not he who had to pay the penalty? She turned away from the wall; it was only an old tale and perhaps had no foundation.

Lured by the beauty of the night, she crossed the lawns and almost without volition her feet led her towards the rose garden. She had reached the gate when the low murmur of voices warned her that she had located the lovers. A tree threw a dense patch of shadow over the gateway, but beyond the paved walks were brightly illuminated, the pool gleaming like a polished mirror reflecting the moonlight. Jessamine and Julian were sitting on the seat where she had sat with him a short while ago, but though close together they were not embracing. Toni felt a swelling sense of outrage that they had chosen that spot, though she had to admit that Julian was unlikely to hold it sacrosanct. Possibly he was seeking to wipe out an embarrassing memory by bringing Jessamine there. The deep shadow concealed her and in the still air she could hear clearly what they were saying. She had not intended to eavesdrop, but catching her own name could not resist the temptation to do so.

Jessamine was saying in her hateful superior voice:

'Toni seems very forward for her age—I suppose that's her Italian blood. As I said before, they mature early and are old women before they're thirty. She isn't a bit like the rest of your family, is she, Ju? She's as dark as a gipsy, except that no gipsy would have such a white skin. It looks unhealthy to me.'

'Toni's healthy enough,' Julian declared. 'She has her mother's colouring. I saw Maria once, but as you say, she'd lost most of her looks and become very stout. I hope Toni doesn't.'

'Perhaps she won't if she diets carefully,' Jessamine said condescendingly, secure in her belief that her own looks were durable. Toni could have cheerfully murdered her. 'Are you wise to encourage her?'

'Encourage her?' Julian sounded astonished.

'Yes, giving her sherry and allowing her to dine with you in that absurd dress that was years too old for her.'

'I don't know where she got it from, but it certainly became her,' Julian said, laughingly. 'She's hardly a baby to be banished to the nursery when we have guests.'

Toni was grateful to him for his championship. He changed the subject, making some remark about the roses, but Jessamine ignored the hint. Toni seemed to have an unholy fascination for her.

'Your cousin—I find it very difficult to realise that she is your cousin—seems to have inherited her mother's temperament as well as her colouring. Girls are supposed to take after their fathers. Does she bear any resemblance to hers at all?'

'I can't say she does, she's certainly a very odd daughter for Lewis to have produced.'

'If he did produce her,' Jessamine insinuated softly, and Toni went rigid with rage. How dared this interloper make such an implication! She went on: 'I mean, these days people are so casual about relationships, and Lewis was an artist, wasn't he?'

Toni fixed anguished eyes on Julian's profile blanched by the moonlight to marble. Surely he would repudiate this monstrous suggestion? To her horror he hesitated, and then admitted:

'I've sometimes wondered.'

'You knew them well, your cousin and his wife?'

'No, I didn't. Lewis was always very cagey about his life in Italy. We hadn't heard from him for years until he wrote a begging letter to Mother saying he was married and a child was on the way. Owing to the fact that the whole district was destroyed by the earthquake it was very difficult to obtain any information about them, though I did eventually secure a record of Toni's birth which we needed. The mother's name was given as Maria Everard, née Rossi, which would seem conclusive.'

'Not necessarily,' Jessamine declared. 'Your cousin might not have known Maria was pregnant when he married her, or he might have done so to give the brat a name. She was his housekeeper, wasn't she?'

'I believe so.' Julian recalled that he had gained the impression that the marriage had been belated. 'But there was really no grounds for such suppositions, Jess. Lewis accepted Antonia as his daughter and we must do likewise, poor child.'

Toni who knew him so well detected the element of doubt in his words and her heart contracted. *He did not believe she was an Everard*, but it had taken Jessamine's jealous spite to make him acknowledge it. Miss Boycott had not liked Julian's unguarded glances and she saw Toni as a possible rival, so she had thought up this method of discrediting her.

'If she's a charity child her airs and graces are most unbecoming,' Jessamine said caustically.

'I hadn't noticed she had any,' Julian returned mildly. Then he added sternly, 'Whatever we surmise it must go no further, Jess. My parents believe she's Lewis's child and I'd hate the girl herself ever to have any inkling that I doubted it.'

'Of course, Ju.' Jessamine bowed her head meekly, but Toni very much doubted that she would keep her surmises to herself. What a mind she must have, Toni thought wrathfully, to be able to think up such an odious explantation of her difference from her kin, and what a slur upon poor Maria who was dead and could not defend herself. Toni could only faintly recall her

76

mother, a large soft presence that had been comfortable and kind, who called her, *'mia bambina, mia carissima'*, in the tender accents of love. Warmth and tenderness seemed to be woefully lacking among the reserved Everards.

Jessamine was speaking again.

'You're very noble, Ju, to do so much for this little Italian by-blow who isn't your kin at all. I only hope you won't regret it. If I'm any judge of character, and I'm quite shrewd, you know, that young madam will put you all to shame before she's finished.'

Toni stayed no longer. She turned away from the rose garden where Jessamine was instilling her poison into Julian's receptive ears and ran blindly away into the moonlit night.

CHAPTER FIVE

THE big wheat field was an moonwashed ocean of stubble with here and there an uncollected bale of straw projecting like a rock from its surface. In one corner the combine lurked like some prehistoric monster. Fleeing from that hateful voice, Toni ran across it, heedless of the sharp spears of corn stalks tearing her tights. At one point she lost her slippers and went on without stopping to look for them. Instinctively she had sought the open country away from the house and grounds where she had been told she had no right to be. 'Charity child.' 'Italian by-blow'—the words continued to ring in her ears, and Julian, instead of denying hotly Jessamine's wicked insinuations, had concurred, expressing his own doubts about her origin. Not only had he repelled her love but he sought to deprive her of her name and home.

Beyond the cornfield was a copse of conifers fringed by undergrowth. Toni pushed her away into their shelter, glad of the shielding darkness. She threw herself down on a bed of pine needles, like a wounded animal seeking cover to lick its wounds.

She was certain herself that Lewis was her father. So often in her infancy he had taken her on his knee and talked to her about Whiteladies, the cradle of her family which one day she must visit, and described to her the gentle Shropshire countryside.

'One day we'll go there together,' he promised her. 'It is your heritage, and who knows? If anything should happen to Julian, and he's a bit of a wild lad, it might become our home.'

Maria would nod her dark head and add: 'Si, si, mia bambina, though our house is poor, you were born inglése madonna.'

They could not have been deceiving her.

After the catastrophe, Julian had told her he was taking her home and his mother would take the place of the one she had lost. He had come immediately to rescue his cousin's orphan and he had no doubt then that she was Lewis's child. Nor during the happy weekends that they had spent together had he had a qualm and he had assisted with her education so that she would be fitted to take her place at Whiteladies as a member of the family.

The change had occurred when he had come back from Saudi Arabia and seen how unlike the Everards she had grown, and her disastrous overtures on Long Mynd had sown the seed of doubt. No English teenager would be so outspoken, so emotionally unrestrained, at least not one that had the background of his family behind her. The encounter in the rose garden had confirmed his suspicions. She was too mature for a product of this chilly climate, too passionate and intense.

Though she had often felt alien from her aunt's way of life, Toni was secretly a little proud of belonging to such a distinguished family, even if it were a little old-fashioned and snobbish. She appreciated that it stood for values and traditions which were regrettably becoming obsolete. She admired and in her better moments sought to imitate. If Julian had come to believe that she was not one of them, it was not surprising he had become cold and distant. Antonia Everard who had no right to her name had become a liability and a menace, a menace because she attracted him physically and was a threat to his integrity, for he considered that a closer union with Toni would be a disaster—for him. Jessamine Boycott with her fair English hair, her good manners and impeccable connections was the kind of girl he wanted to be mistress of Whiteladies and the mother of his children, not an Italian nobody with more temperament than was good for her.

But why did he have to confide his doubts concerning her origins to Jessamine of all people? That was a cruel indignity. Presumably he trusted her discretion, but Toni did not. Jessamine had shown herself capable of being spiteful where she was concerned and could be expected to drop hints. Would Edgar and Linda believe this monstrous suggestion and turn against her too? But at least they were just and there was no proof, moreover they would resent any slur upon the family honour. But Toni was not greatly concerned with their reaction; only Julian's opinion counted with her, and he who knew her best had repudiated her. She felt betrayed by her nearest and dearest.

She crouched against the bole of a tree shivering,

more deeply hurt than when Julian had rejected her love. He had some excuse for that, he still saw her as a child, but this was inexcusable. An owl hooted in the tree above her head, recalling her first night at White-ladies, when Julian had sat on her bed and told her the story of Goldilocks. Why couldn't she have inherited Lewis's fair hair, then there would be no question of his fatherhood, but she was dark as a gipsy except for her 'unhealthy white skin'—Jessamine was expert at plant-ing her darts. 'Girls are supposed to take after their fathers' . . . could Julian possibly be right?

'Oh, why didn't I die in the earthquake too?' she cried aloud, but only the melancholy hoot of the owl answered her.

Jessamine's voice again . . . 'That young madam is likely to put you all to shame.' Had Julian accepted that possibility too? Toni turned hot all over as she re-called their embraces in the rose garden. He had told her then . . . oh, ever so politely . . . that she had wanton urges. He believed they were prompted by her heritage from her mother and an unknown man who had loved not wisely but too well, a heritage he deplored. Poor maligned Maria, who had grown coarse and fat in middle life when Julian met her. Jessamine had im-plied that she would go the same way, a prophecy Julian would regard with distaste. He had been her dearest friend for so many years, her mainstay and her prop, and now for the sake of a strange young woman he had deserted her. Toni covered her face with her hands and wept.

The storm of tears gradually ceased, and she pulled herself together, wiping her face with the edge of Linda's cloak. Tears were useless—who cared how much she wept? Certainly not Julian. As a child when hurt by one it loves cries out, 'I hate you!' and utters threats of impossible vengeance, so Toni's cherished love for Julian changed and she began to weave wild plans to injure him. But whereas a child soon forgets its pain and does not mean what it has said, Toni's reverse of feeling crystallised into a hard knot of resentment. Julian had rent her pride to rags, rejecting her love and doubting her legitimacy, betraying her to her enemy. For that she would one day repay him, but first she must succeed in her profession, and learn not only her trade but all the artifices women use to ensnare a man. She knew she had the power to ignite him which was what had caused him to retreat, but when she had acquired subtlety, she would subjugate him. By then he would in all probability have married Jessamine, but that would be all the worse for him, she decided grimly, for she would have no scruples about breaking up his marriage.

By wile and guile she would bring him to her feet and then she would spurn him, tell him he was a foolish old man, yes, old, old ... she smote the tree bole with her hand. He had made such a point of the difference in their ages, and she would drive it home to humiliate him. She would replace the predominant motive for all her actions, her love for him, by her desire for revenge. Deriving comfort from this somewhat melodramatic plan, she became aware of her surroundings and her physical discomfort. She was cramped and cold from her long vigil, her dress torn, her hair disordered and full of bits of leaf and twig, and her unprotected feet were sore from her wild flight. It must be very late, but she did not think she would have been missed. Her aunt and uncle would believe she had gone to bed and the other two would be too absorbed in each other to wonder what had become of her.

She began to grope her way towards the edge of the

wood. Then she froze as a moving shadow fell across the screening undergrowth. Someone was lurking there, perhaps a poacher. Toni moved stealthily back into the darkness beneath the trees, her heart beating fast. This was not the time and place to be trapped by some strange man, who might be an unsavoury character. Some animal was pushing its way through into the wood —he must have a dog. She saw a dim shaggy shape advancing towards her, and sought for a stick with which to defend herself, but her seeking fingers found nothing except pine needles, and then the beast was upon her uttering yelps of delight. It was Julian's setter.

'Oh, Caesar!' she exclaimed in joy and relief, burying her hands in the dog's silky coat, as he reared up on his hind legs to lick her face. 'But what on earth are you doing here?'

'So he's found you.' The light from a torch swept over her revealing her dishevelment. 'Good God, Toni, what's happened to you?' Julian demanded. 'Caesar, down!'

The dog left her, and went to his master. Toni drew the cloak more closely round her to conceal her torn dress.

'Nothing's happened,' she said haughtily. 'I just came out for a stroll.'

'Do you know what time it is?' he asked. 'It's past midnight. We were worried about you, so I came to look for you.'

'I thought you were too occupied to notice I was missing.'

'Ah, so Mother was right!'

It was too dark to see his face, but he sounded annoyed.

'What do you mean ... right?' she asked uncertainly.

'When she found you weren't in your room nor apparently in the house, she deduced you'd gone off in a fit of pique. Come off it, Toni, you mustn't be so childish.'

'You flatter yourself—what do I care who you're with or what you're doing?' she cried wildly, furious that he should describe her heartbreak as a fit of pique. Moving past him, she ran towards the edge of the wood, trod on a sharp stone and fell prone. Thinking it was some sort of game, Caesar bounded up and again licked her face.

'Pride goes before a fall,' Julian observed unkindly. 'Get up, Toni, it's time you were in bed.'

She tried to struggle to her feet, aware of a sharp stab of pain.

'I ... I've hurt my foot,' she gasped.

He shone the torch over her.

'Not surprising, running about without shoes,' he said grimly. He hauled her up ungently, and she leaned against him while she turned up her foot to look over her shoulder at it. There was a gash across the sole of it oozing blood amid remnants of torn nylon.

'It only wanted that to round off a perfect evening,' Julian exclaimed in exasperation. 'Put your arms round my neck, I'll have to carry you.'

'Why not a fireman's lift? It's less ... intimate.'

'I've no time for cracks now,' he said sharply as he picked her up. 'What you need, my girl, is a good spanking!'

'I'm quite helpless, so now's your opportunity to administer it.'

He gave a half groan as he fought his way out of the undergrowth into the moonlit field. Toni realised he had changed from his dinner clothes into slacks and sweater. Linda must have sent him out to look for her and he was naturally put out at this end to his romantic evening.

'You should have left me to bring myself home,' she told him. 'I'd have come back eventually if I hadn't died in the meantime. I wish I had, then you might be sorry!'

'A typically childish remark, but as you wouldn't be there to witness my grief you wouldn't get any satisfaction out of it.'

'How do you know?' She rubbed her cheek against his chin, her resentment temporarily lulled, now she had got him again to herself. 'Would you mourn for me if I died, Julian, or would it be ... a relief?'

'Don't talk nonsense!' He stopped by one of the bales of straw and dumped her down upon it. Toni felt a thrill of dismay. Was he unchivalrous enough to take her at her word?

'So you're going to abandon me?' she inquired.

'I'm going to tie a handkerchief round that foot of yours, it's dripping,' he returned shortly. 'Luckily I've got a clean one.'

He knelt down to fix the makeshift bandage and Toni, gazing at his bent head, recalled her determination to bring him in homage to her feet, but at that moment he was regarding her as a tiresome child. The handkerchief in place, he made no move to rise, but held her foot in his hand as if it were something precious. She said provocatively:

'In the nursery we always said kiss it better.'

He dropped it as if it were red hot and looked up at her, scowling.

'You're a little wretch, Toni, but you're too big to chastise. I've left it too late. Now would you kindly tell me what you were doing in the wood at this time of night?'

Her lips curled mischievously. 'I had an assignment.'

'Who with?'

She folded her hands demurely in her lap.

'I'm not telling.'

She was not sure whether he believed her or not, but she certainly could not divulge to him of all people the real reason for her headlong flight.

'You might have had the sense to put some boots on,' he scolded.

'Boots are so unromantic,' she sighed.

Julian stood up abruptly and seized her by the shoulders with hands like steel clamps, turning her so that she faced the moonlight.

'Will you please tell me the truth? I don't believe you were meeting a boy. You've always pretended to despise them.'

The glitter in his eyes was visible in the white light. Toni dropped her gaze from his.

'You needn't try your C.I.D. methods on me! You're right, I wasn't meeting anyone. I merely wanted to commune with nature.'

'You've had all day to do that, and it isn't safe to roam about at night alone.' He removed his hands from her shoulders and thrust them into his trouser pockets. 'I hoped—we all hoped Greystones would teach you to be less of a hoyden.'

'They tried,' she informed him with renewed hurt. Who if not himself had encouraged her to be a tomboy. All those excursions together exploring the countryside at night—of course he wanted to forget them now Jessamine was his goal.

'You can't make a silk purse out of a sow's ear,' she pointed out.

'Don't be trite. You could become a most attractive

and charming woman if only you'd try to control your crazy impulses.'

She winced; that was a slap for her uninhibited behaviour in the rose garden. Wanting to hit back, she observed,

'I don't think Jessamine would be pleased if she knew we were enjoying a midnight confrontation in the corn-field, and ...' she waved her bandaged foot ... 'I can't break it off by walking away.'

'Enjoying is hardly the right word,' he returned, then with sudden heat, 'By God, I really will take a stick to you if you don't stop trying to needle me!'

'That would be most exciting,' Toni said calmly, and he muttered an imprecation under his breath.

'But were you really anxious about me?' she went on in softer tone. 'Or did you come to look for me because Zia Linda made you?'

'Of course not. You may be a devil's imp, Toni, but I do care very much what becomes of you.'

Toni was touched by his obvious sincerity. This was the friend to whom she had always taken her troubles. She hesitated, tempted to ask him if he really believed what he had told Jessamine about her mother. She longed to confide in him, but to do so meant that she must admit to eavesdropping. While she hesitated, he said curtly:

'Do you think you could manage to walk the rest of the way? It isn't so far.' He glanced down at the sharp stalks of the stubble. 'No, I suppose you couldn't walk through this stuff. Come on.'

He stopped to lift her, and his reluctance to touch her stung. He was not her friend any longer, he had become critical, censorious, and did not want to carry her because the close contact might drive him into some rash demonstration. Toni's instinct told her they were sexually compatible; if only he would yield to his desires, forget her youth and exploit her dawning womanhood, but he was an Everard, a man of principle who controlled his urges with an iron hand. He considered it would be wrong to take advantage of her youth and innocence, and Everards were disciplined people whose heads ruled their hearts, unlike Italian nobodies who were more passionate than sensible.

Julian strode rapidly across the field, but when he reached the grounds he had perforce to put her down, for Toni was a fair weight. He gently lowered her on to a rustic seat, there were several dotted about the lawns, and wiped his brow with his sleeve. Caesar, who had been foraging in the field, trotted up with an important air and dropped Toni's slippers at her feet, wagging his tail expecting praise. They were soft kid ballerinas with low heels and had been wrenched from her feet during the impetuous rush through the stubble.

'Well done, boy,' Julian said mechanically. He looked at Toni quizzically. 'Yours?'

She picked up a scuffed shoe and put it on her un-injured foot.

'I like running barefoot in the dew,' she said defensively to explain the loss of her footgear. She started to fumble with the knot of his handkerchief.

'Through stubble? What are you doing?'

'I must get this off to get my shoe on.'

'Leave it alone, you'll start the cut bleeding again. I'll be all right when I get my second wind.'

'I'd much prefer to walk.'

'Well, you can't,' he told her irritably. 'As it is you'll probably get blood poisoning. Have you no sense at all?'

'No, only sensibility,' she flashed. 'I hate being a burden to you.' She meant in more senses than one.

'And I'd hate you to lose your foot.' He drew her arms about his neck. 'Come on, it's the last lap.'

Toni relaxed in his arms with a long sigh. So close in body and so apart in spirit. She knew he was with difficulty controlling his annoyance with her foolishness.

Linda wearing her dressing gown, met them at the front door. She had evidently been watching their approach.

'Has Toni had an accident?' she asked anxiously.

'She's been running wild and cut her foot,' Julian replied tersely. 'Caesar found her and I had to carry her.' He made for the stairs. 'I'll put her in her room and then you can attend to her.'

'I'll get the Dettol from the bathroom,' Linda announced, hurrying up ahead of them. Caesar brought up the rear of the little procession. He was not normally allowed upstairs but hoped to escape notice while his master's attention was diverted.

Julian flicked on the light and dropped Toni on her bed. He straightened himself and stood looking down at her with an inscrutable expression. The bright illumination showed the tear stains unrevealed by the moonlight mingled with the dirt on her face.

'Aren't you making heavy weather out of nothing?' he asked sternly. 'You're behaving like a spoilt child that's been denied a toy. Jess and I will always be your friends.'

Toni turned her head away. Friends, after what had been said between them!

Her aunt came in with the disinfectant and a roll of plaster.

'That dog shouldn't be up here,' she remarked.

Toni sat up abruptly.

'Caesar is privileged, but for him I'd have been out all night.'

Julian did not say 'Serve you right,' but his look expressed it. With a curt goodnight he made for the door, whistling to Caesar as he went.

Toni threw off Linda's cloak, thereby shaking a cloud of dust and pine needles on to the floor.

'I took it because it was handy,' she murmured apologetically.

'That's all right, dear.' Linda was examining her foot. 'Things left hanging in the hall are for general use. This is a nasty cut, I'll get some water and bathe it.'

She proceeded to minister to her niece and forbore to lecture. She had told Julian Toni had rushed off in a fit of pique and she had divined part of the girl's trouble. Sensing her unspoken sympathy, Toni had an impulse to throw herself into the older woman's arms and sob out all her anguish and despair, but between her and her great-aunt there had always been a wall of reserve. She was being kind, but if Toni confessed her frustrated love for her son she would only trot out the same old rigmarole about being too young to know her own feelings and she would recover from her girlish fixation in time. Nor did she want to speak of the slur Julian had put upon her birth; she might admit to a similar doubt, which would be devastating.

Her foot dressed, her face washed, Linda helped her to undress and get into bed. Folding the remains of the chiffon dress, she remarked:

'That dress is about done for, but it's no great loss. It didn't really suit you.'

'You mean it makes me look like a tart,' Toni said defiantly.

Linda visibly wilted. 'Please, Toni, where do you pick up such words?'

'They're in common use nowadays,' Toni told her.

Linda sighed. 'This vulgar modern age,' she deplored.

She looked commiseratingly at Toni's pale face on the pillow. 'I understand you must feel a little excluded, dear, after having been such pals with Julian, but it's inevitable he'd want to marry some day. It'll make a difference to me too, but Jessamine is such a nice girl it'll be a pleasure to have her in the family, and you'll have all the exitement of the wedding to look forward too—she's sure to ask you to be her bridesmaid.'

'That will be a consolation,' Toni said, her face like stone. Mrs Everard had not understood at all. 'Goodnight, Zia.'

Linda kissed her forehead. 'Goodnight, dear, sleep well.'

She switched off the light as she went out and Toni stared mutinously into the darkness. Jessamine's bridesmaid, never!

She awoke next morning after a deep sleep; her emotional turmoil of the previous night had exhausted her. The sun was shining through the window—she never drew her curtains at night—making a bright pattern on the floor. She lay for a while, aware of a dark cloud of unhappiness looming over her until she had recalled the previous evening's experiences. She had softened towards Julian when he had carried her home, but now her burning resentment reasserted itself. It was his mother who had been anxious and had sent him in search of her and he had been angered by her escapade. He did not really care what became of her, she insisted, fanning her sense of grievance, though he had pretended otherwise. The only salve for her wounded pride was revenge, and she would have to wait a long time before she was able to implement it. Her eyes fell on the framed photograph of him beside her bed. It always stood there, even at school, where the girls had teased her about it.

'If I hadn't got a boy-friend I wouldn't display a relative,' one girl had said. 'Looks as though you're hard up.'

'You know very well boy-friends' photos aren't allowed in here,' Toni had returned.

Annabel had said Julian was very handsome.

The likeness was a good one, his lips curled in a little mocking smile. Toni stretched out a hand and laid it face down on her bedside table. 'Traitor!' she whispered.

She felt extremely reluctant to get up, go down to breakfast and face Jessamine again, but she was spared that necessity. Linda came in with a tray.

'I thought the foot might be paining you,' she said, 'and you were so late last night. How is it?'

'Oh, Zia, you are kind,' Toni cried gratefully, raising herself on her pillows. 'It's a bit sore, but it'll soon be all right.'

'You don't think we ought to get a doctor to look at it?'

'Good gracious, no. I'll only have an interesting limp for a day or two.'

Linda laid the tray across her knees—coffee, toast, scrambled egg. Toni looked at it and her eyes filled.

'You do care a little for me, Zia Linda?' she asked, longing for reassurance. 'I know I'm awfully tiresome occasionally and I was stupid to go out last night and wear that dress, and ... and ...' Her voice broke.

Mrs Everard laid a tentative hand on her black head. 'I'm very fond of you, dear, like ... a daughter.' Toni noticed the slight hesitation. Linda's daughter would have been vastly different from herself. 'Most of your failings stem from thoughtlessness,' Linda went on. 'When you've learned to control your ... er ... impulsiveness you'll be a very lovable woman, Toni.'

Toni flashed her a mischievous glance. Linda would not mind how lovable she became once Julian was safely married. She might say she was fond of her as a daughter, but she would not appreciate her as a daughter-in-law.

'Thank you,' she said politely. 'How's the blushing bride this morning?'

Linda glanced anxiously over her shoulder. 'Hush, Toni, you mustn't call her that yet. They're going out for the day. Jessamine wants to see something of the country.'

'They've got a nice morning,' Toni observed, eyeing her breakfast dubiously. She did not feel hungry.

The half open door was pushed ajar as Julian came in to ask about her foot. Linda looked slightly put out by his appearance. She considered the intimacy between him and Toni should be checked now the girl was growing up.

'I thought you'd gone, Julian.'

'I wouldn't go without inquiring about our wounded Amazon,' he returned lightly. He looked attractive in casual slacks and blue shirt, the latter matching his eyes.

'Nice of you not to rub in that it was my own fault,' Toni remarked, not looking at him. Knowing that he was off for the day with Jessamine hurt much more than her foot did. 'I'll be hobbling around by the time you get back.'

'Well, don't overdo it.'

'Jessamine will be waiting,' Linda said pointedly, as he seemed disposed to linger.

'Yes, of course. 'Bye, Toni, be good.'

'Go carefully!' she called as he closed the door behind him.

Appropriately the sun went behind a cloud, the brightness fading from the room.

They returned just before the dinner hour, by which time the day had become overcast with a threat of rain, so there would be no roaming in the gloaming that night, Toni thought with satisfaction. She was managing to move about with the aid of a stick and a thick pad under the sole of her foot. She had thought of saying that she could not get downstairs so that she would not have to encounter Jessamine, but she soon became bored with her own room and decided that such avoidance would not only be cowardly but would leave the field clear for her enemy. For dinner she put on a black crêpe dress that Linda had bought her for evening wear, hoping to subdue her striking appearance, but it only served to enhance her white skin and dusky hair. Jessamine wore a long gown in pink silk, very décolletée. Toni thought it made her look ordinary. She glanced at Miss Boycott's left hand, but it was still ringless. It transpired that Julian had taken her to Church Stretton and over the Long Mynd. Involuntarily Toni flashed a reproachful look towards him. She had regarded the Mynd as their special place. Jessamine, who had been describing it enthusiastically, broke off to say:

'But of course you all know it better than I do.'

'Julian and I were up there some weeks back,' Toni told her carelessly. 'We were celebrating his return from the East.' This time her glance was challenging and he met it with a cold stare.

'How nice,' Jessamine remarked, sensing an undercurrent.

'It wasn't at all nice. We had a misunderstanding,' Toni went on recklessly. 'However, we went off to Much Wenlock and drowned our differences in cups of tea. I suppose he took you there to exorcise my ghost.'

'Do talk sense, Toni!' Julian bade her sharply, and Toni knew by the glint in his eyes that she had touched him. 'Jess wanted to see something of the country and that's the most spectacular place in the locality.'

'You needn't explain,' Toni returned. 'I quite understand.'

Jessamine was eyeing her dress, which she thought was much too old for her, but could not decide what would be a suitable garb to eclipse that black and ivory beauty. Teenagers had no business to look so alluring, it encouraged them to be impertinent. Julian turned his attention to her with marked deliberation and Toni was silent for the rest of the meal. Afterwards she excused herself, saying she must rest her foot, and went up to her room. She could no longer bear to watch them together.

Jessamine was a keen sportswoman; she rode to hounds, played games and even shot. On her second and last night at dinner, having spent the day in Shrewsbury with Julian, it transpired that she was trying to persuade him to join her in Scotland where she would be staying with friends during September.

'I've told him there's plenty of grouse,' she informed the table at large, 'and he might even get a chance to shoot a stag. Surely that's an inducement.'

Julian said a little shortly that he would be back at work by then.

'Surely you could get time off?' she insisted. Then she burst out eagerly: 'Why don't you resign? I'm sure Mr Everard,' she smiled at Edgar, 'would be glad to have you at home. It's such a big place to run single-handed.'

This suggestion was received in silence. It was something that had often been discussed without reaching a conclusion. They all looked at Julian, whose face was expressionless. Then his father cleared his throat and declared:

'I've always wanted Julian to live his own life independent of family ties. I hope he will take over here eventually, but there's no hurry. I can carry on for a long while yet.'

'But it's a much better life than messing about in the oil business,' Jessamine insisted, and Toni saw an angry flush mount to Julian's brow. He enjoyed his work and Jessamine was foolish to decry it.

'I'd love to live here,' the other girl concluded.

'Perhaps you will, one day,' Julian told her, 'but I make my own decisions.'

'Of course, dear,' Jessamine agreed, realising she had gone too far.

When next day Julian returned from seeing her off, Linda inquired hopefully:

'Are we to take it that you're engaged?'

They were having tea when he came in and he looked at his mother moodily, as he sat down.

'I haven't proposed yet. Perhaps she'll refuse me.'

Toni glanced at him quickly, then turned away her head. Something must have gone wrong.

'I'm sure she won't,' Edgar declared heartily, 'but don't hesitate too long, my boy, she may get tired of waiting.'

They were all eager for this match, Toni thought bitterly, except, oddly enough, Julian himself, who seemed to be stalling.

'I daresay it'll be settled when I join her in Scotland,' he told them, but without enthusiasm. His eyes were on Toni's profile, cameo-clear against the wall behind her. Looking round she asked maliciously:

'So you couldn't resist the grouse and the stag?'

'They were no inducement. I don't shoot except with a camera.' Both he and Toni disliked blood sports, but she thought Jessamine might have converted him. As his mother handed him a cup of tea, Toni said cuttingly:

'Your beloved will think you're a cissy.'

'Toni!' Linda expostulated. 'That's an unkind thing to say. Jessamine will understand that Julian only kills in self-defence.' Toni raised sceptical brows. 'She'd never think he's a cissy.'

'I'm quite indifferent to Jessamine's opinion of me,' Julian announced, which was a peculiar assertion for a prospective fiancé to make.

'That's right, don't let her dictate to you,' Edgar approved, handing him the bread and butter. 'Begin as you mean to go on, a man should be master in his own house.'

Julian and Linda exchanged amused glances. Both knew whose was the ruling hand at Whiteladies, and it was not Edgar's.

'I object to having my future decided for me,' Julian explained.

'You can't blame her for wanting to settle down,' his mother defended the absent Jessamine anxiously.

Julian shrugged his shoulders, his eyes again on Toni.

'Well, I'll be in London when the great announcement is made,' she said lightly, thankful that she would miss the rejoicings over the engagement. She had not thought Julian was in love with Jessamine, not as she understood love, but his present abstracted manner and glumness could only be interpreted as depression over his girl's departure.

'Oh, but you must come home for the engagement party,' her aunt declared.

Julian smiled sardonically. 'Got it all taped, haven't you, Mum?'

'Well, you *have* rather committed yourself,' she pointed out.

Julian turned his head away. 'I suppose I have, but it'll be some time before you can have your party.'

'I'll need time,' she said gaily. 'There'll be a great many preparations to make. When do you go to Scotland?'

He shrugged his shoulders. 'The date isn't fixed yet.'

Julian did not go to Scotland, nor was there an engagement party. To the dismay and consternation of his parents he announced that he had accepted an assignment in Africa and would be away for several years.

CHAPTER SIX

TONI's rise to stardom was meteoric. In a profession where so much depends upon being in the right place at the right time, her luck was phenomenal. When her course ended at R.A.D.A. she was snapped up by a television company to play the juvenile lead in a series dealing with the last days of Pompeii. She had the voice, face and figure for the part, that of a classic Italian, and a hint of sulphurous underlying emotions that they required. Mrs Thorne was a friend of the director and brought Toni to his notice. After he had seen her in the end-of-term Academy production she was signed up forthwith, her lack of experience being outweighed by her other assets. Thus the beautiful face of Antonia Alderly, as she called herself, became familiar to several million viewers and her presentation of the part more than fulfilled expectations. Annabel was jubilant.

'I knew it, you've got it all,' she exclaimed triumphantly, 'and so did Ma. She's become quite reconciled to my speech therapy now she's got you to push, and you're much more rewarding. I never had much talent.'

Toni smiled, her Mona Lisa smile that had become famous, for success was secondary to her real objective, but that had to lie in abeyance until Julian returned from Africa. Meanwhile other engagements followed and she was developing fast, acquiring a poise and assurance far beyond her years. She was indifferent alike to the jealousy of her colleagues who resented her sudden rise, and the admiration of her fans, among whom were many presentable males. Occasionally she went out with one of them, returning from such assignments with a still more enigmatical smile and apparently unscathed. She went because she wanted to learn how to handle men, and chose experienced types for that purpose. Some, finding her unavailable, did not repeat their invitations. others became intrigued and continued their attentions until, becoming bored with them, she dropped them. One who survived as her favoured escort was a Lord Greenough, a wealthy and polished man about town with a doubtful reputation. Although in his forties he was still slim and elegant with an aquiline aristocratic face. Although he did not disguise the fact that his ultimate aim was seduction, Toni encouraged him, she felt she could learn a lot from him.

Mrs Thorne viewed this development with alarmed disapproval.

'He's a roué and a rake,' she declared emphatically. 'He's no use to you, Toni, he'd never dream of marrying you.'

'I've no intention of marrying anyone,' Toni returned. 'As for Ambrose, he amuses me and he's most instructive.'

'My dear girl, do be careful. He's notorious,' Mrs Thorne continued to protest.

'Which makes him exciting,' Toni said coolly. 'Don't worry, Mrs Thorne, I can handle him. Don't I deserve a little fun after all my hard work? He takes me to the best restaurants and tells me all I should know about food and drink, besides advising me how to dress. Of course I'm not such a fool as to go to his flat.'

'I should hope not!' her monitress ejaculated, deciding Toni was becoming too much of a responsibility. Should she warn her aunt about her conduct? But she did not like telling tales and in the end did nothing.

Lord Greenough, whatever he hoped finally to achieve, liked being seen about with the beautiful young actress who flattered him with her deference to his tuition. Under his guidance she learned to avoid the flamboyant and dress quietly but stylishly. His cynical and often cruel remarks about other women amused her. He took her whenever she was free to many outstanding events—first nights, Ascot, Henley, and once when she had a free weekend to Cowes Regatta, but he often grumbled when she had to leave him because of her work.

'You're a queen bee, not a drone,' he told her. 'Say the word and I'll give you your own establishment and one that'll be the right setting for you. A palace in Italy or an island in the Caribbean, where you'll never have to do anything except look lovely and laze in the sun.'

'Thanks for the kind thought, but I'd be bored to death,' Toni returned.

'Not with me to entertain you.'

She shook her dark head. 'I'll be no man's mistress, Ambrose.'

But his interest in her was more than amorous; he enjoyed assisting with her development, and as he was a cultivated man the association was beneficial to her. He would have given her jewels, but she would take nothing from him except entertainment, which she considered she repaid with her company.

She was becoming a little irritated by Mrs Thorne's supervision, ineffectual though it was, and decided that as soon as she attained her majority she would invest in a place of her own. Bayswater where the Thornes lived was central, but the flat was too small for her expanding ego and she wanted to be able to entertain her friends.

Then through Mrs Thorne's good offices she obtained the part of Eliza Doolittle in a revival of Bernard Shaw's *Pygmalion* upon the West End stage.

'She is a little like Mrs Pat Campbell, you know,' Mrs Thorne had pointed out, referring to the actress for whom the part had been originally written.

'I hope G.B.S. isn't turning in his grave,' Toni said to Annabel. 'I'm sure there's no comparison between me and his Stella.'

But after she was tried out in the part, she was immediately engaged. This for a girl not yet twenty was a tremendous achievement, but Toni had always seemed older than her years. Jessamine's spiteful remarks about ripening early and losing her bloom sometimes troubled her, and she would study her face and figure anxiously for any sign of deterioration, but she never put on weight, she lived so intensely she burned up all surplus fat, and her features seemed to become more sculptured as she grew older.

Her leading man in the play was called Oliver Ranworth, a big shambling person with a clever hatchet face, a polished technique and a world-wide reputation as an actor. He had started by resenting her, declaring that it was an insult to be expected to play opposite a novice, but rehearsals were only half way through before he succumbed to her charm and beauty. She was, he declared, unique, a genius and not to be judged by ordinary standards, which did not endear her to the other women in the company. He too was over forty and Toni encouraged him delicately with the new technique of advance and withdrawal that she had learned with Ambrose. All men were material to practise upon, until Julian returned.

There had been no weekly letters upon this occasion; he was somewhere in Africa and several months elapsed before Toni had any word from him at all. Then he did write, a friendly, slightly formal epistle describing the locality and asking for news of her. Restraining her first impulse to reply at once, Toni allowed several weeks to go by before answering. Then she gave him an account of her various film engagements with brilliant little pen sketches of the odd characters she met, giving the impression that she was absorbed in her new life and only wrote to him out of cousinly duty. Thereafter they maintained an intermittent correspondence, but he never mentioned Jessamine Boycott, nor did Toni inquire about her. What had transpired between him and her she did not know. She found her aunt and uncle seemed under the impression that they wrote to each other and Jessamine was waiting for him to complete his assignment, when they would marry and take over Whiteladies—a supposition Toni thought was more founded upon wishful thinking than upon fact, for Julian's flight to Africa seemed more like an escape from both his bride and his home responsibilities. But he had been gone for several years and was due home soon, when something would have to be resolved.

The opening night of *Pygmalion* was a big occasion for Toni, being her debut on the West End stage, and she went down to the theatre to prepare for it in a state of nervous apprehension. She was still very young and inexperienced, and though the play had gone well in rehearsal and Oliver had been fulsome in his praise it remained to be seen if she could put the part across to a sophisticated audience, to say nothing of the critics. She had many famous predecessors in the role, including the stars of the musical made from it. The comparisons might not be in her favour.

Arriving early at the theatre, she saw the queues already collected with a vague surprise, people who had come to see her perform. The lights above the entrance spelt out her name and Oliver's. She felt a thrill when she saw them for the first time. The Everards had come up from Shropshire to spend a couple of nights in London so they could see the play and Annabel and her mother were determined that Toni could not fail. She only hoped they were right. She had met her aunt and uncle for lunch and learned from them that Julian was on his way home. It was more than ever important that he should be greeted with the news of her success. She wondered if he were much changed—older, of course, but not so old as Oliver, who considered he was quite young enough to be her lover. At least Julian could no longer treat her as a child.

The doorkeeper, a somewhat dour old man, unbent enough to wish her luck as she went through the stage door. Her dressing room was gay with flowers; Oliver, the Thornes and various Academy colleagues had sent them. A few telegrams were stuck round the mirror in the traditional manner, but not many, as they had become too expensive. Her dresser, a coloured woman named Ellen Smithson, had set out her make-up on a towel before the mirror. She was a motherly soul, and had already developed a devotion to Toni. It crossed the girl's mind that when she rented her flat, Ellen might come to live with her and attend to her needs. She hung up Toni's dress on a hanger as the girl discarded it and helped her into a wrap, tying a scarf over her hair as she sat down in front of the glass preparatory to making up.

Toni sifted through the small pile of letters and cards neatly stacked beside her cosmetics. She had hoped there might be a word from Julian, who had been told of her opening date; he might at least have wished her luck, but there was nothing. His thoughts would be turning towards Jessamine, she reflected bitterly, if his parents assumption was right, and he would be anxious to keep his distance now he was coming back. She wondered how she was going to contact him, for it was no part of her plans to allow him to ignore her.

She studied her face in the mirror before applying the foundation cream. The liquid dark eyes under the broad white brow stared back at her from its crystal depths. Though she was not yet twenty and the contours of her chin and jaw retained their youthful curve, her eyes had lost their look of candid innocence. One could not live amid the hectic world of the theatre or associate with men like Lord Greenough without acquiring knowledge of the ways of the world and the weaknesses of mankind. She decided with satisfaction that they had acquired instead depth and mystery. Her face was a little too thin, causing her eyes to look enormous, and her body was slender as a reed. So much for Jessamine's prophecies! Recalling Julian's lean lithe figure, Toni smiled faintly, thinking, 'I must be an Everard after all.'

When she was made up Ellen helped her to put on the rough blouse, skirt, shawl and straw hat of the flower girl that she was in her first appearance. Toni could play the gamine as effectively as the duchess. With the costume her features seemed to sharpen and acquire the impertinent air of the street urchin, as she said with her carefully studied cockney accent:

'Cross my 'eart, but I look a proper slut!'

The woman laughed, 'Best of luck, miss,' as the tannoy called for 'Orchestra and beginners.'

Toni smiled wanly and thanked her. Her heart was beating fast and she felt deadly sick. She would not be a true artiste if she did not suffer from nerves, but she knew from experience that they would vanish as soon as she stepped on to the stage.

There was a full house. Oliver had his following if she had not ... yet ... and his Professor Higgins was one of his star parts. Before the play was half way through Toni's success was assured. At Mrs Higgins' tea-party where the newly created Eliza makes her debut, she looked beautiful and regal, though the once famous exit line had lost most of its impact in these days of freer speech. In the final act where she tells the Professor what she thinks of him for meddling with her life, she was reminded again of Julian. He had meant well, but he had not realised what he was doing when he allowed her to attach herself wholeheartedly to him. Her devotion had flattered him, but he had thought no more of it than he would that of a puppy.

After the curtain calls, which were many, Oliver took her in his arms as she came off the stage to where he was waiting for her.

'You were stupendous darling, absolutely marvellous!

Tonight a star was born,' he declared fatuously, and kissed her soundly. They were standing in the wings and looking over his shoulder in the direction of her dressing room, Toni saw Julian. She had no idea that he had been in front, but he must have been, for he was wearing evening dress, which a few first-nighters still did out of compliment to the players and the management. She did not even know that he had arrived in London. But more than his unexpected appearance, his expression startled her. For a second she saw naked fury in his face, while his eyes glittered, then his normal urbane mask descended and he looked slightly bored. Becoming aware that she was still in Oliver's arms, Toni pushed the actor away and moved towards Julian.

'Why, Julian, what a surprise!' she greeted him. 'But what are you doing here? Have you lost your way?' She held out her hand.

'I was looking for your dressing room,' he explained, barely touching her fingers. 'I wanted to be the first to congratulate you, but it seems I was forestalled.'

'But you are—Oliver's one of the cast so he doesn't count. Come along, we mustn't linger here getting in the way.'

She was conscious that both men were eyeing each other aggressively over her head. Julian could not have timed his entrance better. He had seen Oliver embracing her ardently and he did not like it. Toni became radiant as she led him towards her dressing room while Oliver, murmuring, 'See you later,' went reluctantly to his.

'I saw Zia and Uncle Edgar at lunch time,' Toni remarked as they reached it. 'They didn't say you were expected today.'

'They didn't know. I got an earlier flight and when I phoned Whiteladies from the airport I was told they'd come to town. I called at their hotel and they persuaded me to come along tonight. The theatre was booked solid, but I managed to get a returned seat.'

'I'm sorry you had to be persuaded to come,' Toni said archly.

'Well, theatres aren't much in my line,' he said apologetically, 'and I'd only just arrived. But I'm very glad I did come.'

They looked at each other curiously. Toni saw that he was even browner and leaner than when he went away, but now there were definite lines about his mouth. He wore his evening clothes easily, although they must be an unusual garb for him, and there was an assurance and dignity about him that gave him distinction. The Everards were after all aristocrats, and he looked one. For his part he was regarding her with an intensity that she hoped meant approval and she made a mock curtesy.

'Do I pass muster?'

'I'll like you better when you've got that muck off your face.'

'My warpaint.' She laughed a little vexedly; she had hoped for a compliment. 'That'll soon be done.'

Then a tide of congratulatory friends and relatives came pouring in and they were swept apart. Toni wondered how he had managed to get to her ahead of them—bribed the doorkeeper, perhaps; Julian was a man who knew how to get where he wanted to be when he wanted. What caused her eyes to shine triumphantly was that he had won his way through to her. She had lured him from the auditorium to her side without waiting to escort his relatives or greet his friends. Nor was there any sign of Jessamine. Mrs Thorne was loudly proclaiming that she had always known Toni's potential and tonight she had justified all her efforts on her behalf.

'I'm very grateful to you for everything,' Toni thanked her sincerely.

Mr and Mrs Everard were a little overwhelmed by her success. Edgar kissed her tentatively, getting a mouthful of make-up, and said he was proud of her. Linda whispered that it was such a shame Lewis was dead. He would have felt his existence had been crowned by begetting such a daughter. Poor Lewis, who had always been a failure.

Her words indicated that she had never had any doubts about Toni's parentage. Toni's face hardened as she sought to meet the eyes of the one who had. Julian was leaning negligently against the wall watching all these effusions a little scornfully. Toni wondered why he lingered; he had said his piece and if he were waiting for his parents, there was more room in the corridor.

When Ellen started to shoo everyone away, saying that Miss Alderly wanted to change, he came up to her.

'Come and have supper with me.'

It was more a command than an invitation. Toni thrilled as she always did when he became the dominating male, but he had yet to learn that she was much in demand and could not be expected to be free to yield to his sudden whims.

'I'm so sorry, Julian, but I've promised Oliver,' she returned. The actor had asked her, but she had declined his invitation. Julian would not know that.

His eyes glinted, she had not remembered they were so intensely blue. How attractive they were in the dark tan of his face!

'Is that the lengthy gawk who was kissing you?' he demanded.

'My leading man,' she reproved him. 'He's famous, you know.'

'I'm surprised to hear it,' he remarked drily. 'But you're coming with me. Damn it all, girl, didn't I find you, help educate you, support you in your wish to go on the stage? Where would you be but for me?' It was the first time that he had ever mentioned that she was beholden to him, and her eyes widened in surprise. Ellen shuffled her flat feet, her wide face a circle of remonstrance. At this rate she would never catch her last bus.

'You can tell your leading man,' Julian went on, his eyes mocking her, 'that I'm only spending one night in London, so I'm privileged. He'll have you for the rest of the run.'

'In that case I'll come,' she agreed. 'Now please let me get changed.'

'I'll be at the stage door with a taxi waiting.'

'You wish to send a message to Mr Ranworth?' Ellen asked, when he had gone.

Toni laughed. 'No need, I wasn't going with him. That was what you might call boosting my value.' Her eyes glowed with excitement.

The woman's dark eyes gleamed slyly. 'He's the better man,' she observed as she hung up Toni's last act dress. 'You take that one, yes?'

'He's my cousin,' Toni told her.

'That's no barrier, miss.'

'No, but there are others.'

'Love will always find a way,' Ellen announced sentimentally.

Love? But Julian had killed her love for him by doubting their kinship. That had never been a barrier, but he had created the others. Tonight, if she had learned anything about men, he would attempt to pull them down. She had seen desire in his eyes, but she had erected another one, comprised of wounded pride and her wish to be even with him. He was going to discover she was no longer a naïve teenager compliant to his demands.

Toni put on a black silk dress with a draped neckline that enclosed her body like a sheath. With it she wore a string of cultured pearls, her aunt and uncle's last Christmas gift to her. Her face was almost colourless. Looking at the stark black and white image she presented, she took a red rose from one of her bouquets and pinned it to her bosom. She had worn a red rose on the night of her greatest humiliation, she would wear another to celebrate what she hoped might be a triumph. Ellen helped her on with her fur coat, not mink but humble rabbit disguised as coney seal. It was a chilly night.

Julian took her to a select restaurant where the tables were set in alcoves, thus providing some privacy. She was surprised that he knew such a place, and he was obviously known there, for the proprietor came to speak to him and say how glad he was to see him back again. Seated opposite to him in the discreet lighting, Toni thought Julian looked only little older than when she had first known him. He wore well and was as slim and lithe as he had been as a young man. She found him devastatingly attractive with his quiet air of breeding accentuated by the elegant fit of his evening clothes. Compared with him Oliver appeared uncouth.

'How was Africa?' she asked.

'Hot, and I've landed in the middle of an English winter,' he smiled wryly. 'I'll have to get used to the British climate again, for I've finished with tropical countries. I'll go no more a-roving.'

'You've really come home for good? Uncle Edgar will be pleased.'

'Yes. The old man hasn't been so well lately. Heart's a bit dickey.'

Toni felt concerned. 'Zia Linda never told me.'

'She wouldn't want to bother you.'

'Oh, but she should. I'll worry if I think I'm being kept in the dark.'

'Well, he seemed fine tonight,' Julian pointed out.

Toni looked down at her plate. 'And Jessamine, how is she?' she asked negligently. 'Do you still keep in touch?'

'Yes, she's been a faithful correspondent. I'll have to look her up.' He looked faintly embarrassed. 'She's treated me better than I deserve, for I didn't behave very well. I expect I'll end by marrying her—I might do worse.'

'You might,' Toni agreed, pleased by his lack of enthusiasm. He certainly was not in love with Jessamine. 'Everyone says she's such a nice girl,' she went on, looking at Julian from under her lashes, 'but nice girls can be a little dull.'

Julian met her glance with a glint in his eyes.

'God, Toni, you'd never be dull. Some lucky devil's going to have a most exciting wife.'

'If I ever decide to marry, which I doubt,' Toni told him, beginning to enjoy herself. 'And perhaps he wouldn't be so lucky. I'm temperamental and un-domesticated. I'm not much good at cooking, and burnt offerings don't promote marital harmony.'

'A man can always employ a housekeeper to do the chores.'

'If he can afford one as well as a wife, but in that case, why marry? Housekeepers can be very . . . accommodating.'

110

'I'm surprised at you, Toni!' He pretended to be shocked.

'One learns about life in a theatre, though I wasn't exactly ignorant when I started.'

Julian looked troubled. 'This man, this actor type, is he trustworthy?'

'Not in the least, but I can manage him,' she said coolly. Then noticing his frown, 'Don't worry about me, I'm of age now and I know how to look after myself.'

'All the same ...' He hesitated, then burst out angrily, 'You're so beautiful, Toni, and vulnerable. You oughtn't to be allowed out on your own without a protector.'

She laughed merrily. 'What would you like to do about that? Keep me locked up?'

He grinned wickedly. 'Yes, in a place where only I held the key.'

Toni laughed again. Julian was actually flirting with her!

'That would be terribly monotonous ... for me.'

Julian passed his hand over his brow as if to eradicate some disturbing vision and said in a changed voice:

'I oughtn't to be talking to you like this, but you're a witch, Toni. You'd give any man ... ideas. That's why I'm afraid for you.'

'You needn't be, I assure you I'm not in the least vulnerable.' She put her elbows on the table and rested her chin upon her clasped hands, gazing at him out of dark limpid eyes. 'To be vulnerable, Julian, one has to be deeply involved, but no one can touch my heart, in fact I'm not sure I've got one in the romantic sense. It atrophied long ago. I'm only interested in men as an amusement.'

'You're talking absolute rubbish,' he declared vehemently, averting his eyes from hers. 'With your temperament you can't be cold, you're so young you're simply unawakened.'

She smiled faintly. 'You of all people should know better than that!'

He looked uncomfortable as he recalled past episodes between them.

'You must have grown out of that childish nonsense,' he said tersely.

Toni made no comment, but continued to smile, concealing the sudden rage his words had roused in her. Childish nonsense indeed! He had broken her heart. Well, she had warned him, and he had refused to heed the red light. Now she would set herself to hurt him if she could.

'You're still living with Mrs Thorne?' he asked, changing the subject. 'Are you comfortable?'

'Up to now,' Toni told him, 'but I think the time has come to move on. I want to get a place of my own.'

'Won't that be very expensive? Your work is a little uncertain, isn't it?'

'I'm fairly well established now. *Pygmalion* is only to have a short run, but already I've had tentative offers of another engagement, and I can get heaps of film work—I happen to be exceedingly photogenic. You'll see me quite often on television.'

He scowled and said jealously; 'I don't care for you being sort of public property.'

'Don't be absurd, it's my bread and butter.' A plan was forming for maintaining contact with him. 'Will you be coming up to town, or do you intend to bury yourself in Shropshire?'

'Not entirely, and I think I ought to keep an eye on you from time to time in ... er ... an avuncular capacity.'

'But you're not my uncle,' she told him deliberately. 'I could do with your help in finding a flat.'

He moved restlessly. 'There are agents ...'

'But I've no head for business, Julian, I'm sure to get into an awful mess without an adviser, and I can't stay where I am. Mrs Thorne has been very kind, but she's getting a bit tired of having me around.'

This last was an exaggeration, but Toni was determined to launch out on her own, and she meant to make Julian assist her.

He made some further protests, but she played the role of the helpless litle girl at the mercy of property sharks so convincingly that he began to weaken.

'I'll have to put things in order at Whiteladies first,' he told her. 'I suppose you can wait a few weeks, and then I'll be at your service.'

'Oh, thank you, Julian. You're the only person I can turn to since Uncle Edgar isn't well and my own people are dead.'

He looked at her black and white beauty curiously.

'Lewis certainly hatched a cuckoo when he bred you!'

A remark that stabbed her, for she was sure he was again wondering if Lewis could have been her father.

'That's not a good metaphor,' she declared. 'A cuckoo is a usurper who ends by ruling the roost. I'll never do that. I feel more like a poppy in the corn, a scarlet blot among the golden Everards. A poppy is a weed, decorative but no use to anybody.' There was a note of bitterness in her lovely voice, and Julian raised his eyebrows.

'Your metaphor is more inappropriate than mine. A weed indeed! You're more like a bird of paradise among a flock of sparrows.'

'Wonderful, Julian, what a flight of fancy! I suppose your Jessamine is like a dove?'

'If you mean that as a compliment it isn't. Anyone

who has to do with doves knows they're particularly spiteful birds.'

'I beg your pardon, my natural history is at fault.' But Jessamine was spiteful. 'This particular bird wants her own nest, Julian. You will help me to find it?'

'But you can't live alone,' he protested.

'Oh, I've got that covered. My dresser Ellen is a most capable woman. She'll be glad to look after me.'

She had not sounded Ellen yet and hoped she would agree.

'She's quite respectable?'

'Oh, very,' Toni said emphatically, and wondered if she were right. She did not actually know very much about Ellen Smithson.

They discussed details and Julian said that if they found suitable premises that were unfurnished he was sure there were lots of bits and pieces put away at Whiteladies that she could have.

'Thank you,' Toni was enthusiastic. 'I knew I could rely on you. You compensate for having no father.'

'I'm hardly old enough to be your father,' he pointed out a little curtly.

'But you've always made such a thing of your seniority,' she told him, her eyes dancing impishly. He had forgotten he had talked about being avuncular.

'The gap narrows as we grow older.'

'Do you really think so?' she asked ingenuously. She was progressing! Soon she would have him where she wanted him.

'Well, don't you?'

'I never acknowledged that there was a gap,' she retorted. 'A woman's as old as she looks and a man as he feels. Do you feel young tonight, Julian?'

'I don't think I dare.'

'Rubbish, you'd dare anything.'

'I chose the wrong word,' he sighed. 'I mean I can't afford to be too impetuous. I suppose you've a host of admirers who really are young?'

'I prefer the ones who are getting on a bit,' she admitted frankly. 'I'm expensive, you know, and the youngsters haven't the cash to entertain me adequately.'

Julian stared at her aghast. 'I'd never have believed you could become mercenary, Toni.'

'I'm not, but when one isn't in love one might as well settle for the best provider.' She wondered what he would have made of Lord Greenough. She could imagine his disapproval.

Julian gave her a long searching look, and what he saw seemed to reassure him, for his face cleared and he said mischievously:

'Then since you've become a gourmet I hope your meal tonight fulfilled your expectations.'

'More than,' she assured him, but she was not referring to the food. 'When can we start house-hunting?'

'I told you not for a little while, but you leave it all to me, I'll find you something.'

'I meant it to be a joint search.'

'I'm sure you haven't much time to spare.'

Annoyed because he wanted to defraud her of his company, she said provocatively:

'I hope you won't be too long about it, I do need somewhere to entertain my friends! ... especially my men friends.'

'If you think I'm going to help you to do that ...'

'Entertain my friends? Of course not, but I'll allow you to vet the gentlemen and tell me which ones are dangerous.'

She was all sparkling provocation and Julian's eyes narrowed to slits of blue flame.

'They'll all be dangerous ... You've got what turns men on.'

'Have I really?' She clasped her hands ecstatically. 'I've always wanted to be a femme fatale. Do I turn you on?'

He turned his head away. 'I'm not going to flirt with you, you little menace, but as I've said, I'll get your flat. It must be in a decent neighbourhood with respectable neighbours.' She made a face. 'I think I know someone who can help. Will you want to entertain the shaggy bear?'

'Of course.' She knew better than to allow Oliver to visit her alone, but she sensed that Julian was jealous of the actor and he was too valuable a weapon to discard. 'Is it upon his account that you don't want me to live alone?'

'His and others. You've a reputation to lose.'

'Have I? According to the Sunday papers an actress's reputation is enhanced by lovers.'

But she had gone too far, for Julian looked displeased. 'I wish you wouldn't talk like that, Toni, it's cheap.'

'Now you sound like your mother, but don't worry, I'll only ask Oliver when I'm having a party.' She drew herself up proudly. 'I'll always behave as befits an Everard.'

His face did not change, though she had made this grandiloquent assertion with intention. Had he forgotten he had denied she was one? .

'I hope you will,' he said gravely, and looked at his watch. 'It's very late and you must be tired after all the excitement. I'll take you home in a taxi.'

He helped her on with her coat, and taking her elbow piloted her out of the restaurant. The remaining diners watched their exit with interest. The tall distinguished-looking man and the slim slip of a girl with the arresting face made a striking couple.

'Are you dying to see the morning papers?' Julian asked as they drove through the brightly lit streets. 'I understand performers always are after a first night.'

'They can wait,' Toni returned carelessly, adding with great sweetness, 'much more important than the play is your return, Julian.'

She felt him stiffen beside her and her anger rose. Could she never make an advance without being rebuffed? There had been moments during supper when she had believed he was softening towards her, but now he was putting up his defences again.

'That's a very pretty thing to say, but I can hardly believe it's genuine,' he returned. 'Don't waste your time flattering me, my dear.'

The barriers were definitely up.

Mrs Thorne and Annabel had waited up for her and Annabel came rushing to the door as soon as she heard Toni's key in the lock.

Julian refused to come in, it was late, and he had asked the taxi to wait. The two girls watched him walk away.

'Well, was he at your feet?' Annabel asked as she closed the door.

'Why should he be? He's only a cousin,' Toni replied. To herself she appended, Not yet, but he will be.

CHAPTER SEVEN

THE critics were on the whole kind to Antonia Alderley. 'A great talent not yet fully developed,' and 'This young actress has enormous potential,' were among the most discerning. All of them praised her looks. Toni read her notices almost with indifference, for though her theatrical future seemed assured, fame was not her goal. She was in a fever to see Julian, but he did not come to London again so that all her scheming for a joint house-hunting project seemed to have miscarried. In his preoccupation with the affairs of Whiteladies her needs were shelved.

Christmas came and went. With a performance on Christmas Eve and an extra matinee on Boxing Day, it was impossible for her to go away and she spent a quiet Christmas Day with the Thornes. She sent presents to the three in Shropshire and received gifts in return from her aunt and uncle. Julian sent a card saying his offering would follow in the New Year, but it was to be a surprise. Toni was not much interested; she wanted his presence, not a sop by way of a belated Christmas present. She considered ringing him up to inquire what he was doing about finding a new residence for her, but pride restrained her. If Julian did not want to help her, she would manage on her own; she knew that he would prefer that she stayed where she was, but that she was resolved not to do.

Ellen Smithson received her suggestion that she might housekeep for her with delight. It transpired she had been married, but her husband had deserted her and she worked not only to keep herself but to help her parents who lived in Notting Hill. She had a daughter, a teenage girl who had just started work as an office girl, who lived with her grandparents, and Toni promised that Melissa, as she was called, should visit her mother as often as she pleased when she was settled. She was a coffee-coloured youngster, with a mass of dense black hair. She regarded Toni with wide-eyed wonder, overawed by the glamour of actually meeting an actress she had seen on the screen.

Toni gave her a lavish present of clothes for Christmas, going shopping with Ellen for that purpose. It made her feel that she had some sort of family. The Smithsons' choice of gear was a little garish, but she was determined that Melissa should have what she fancied. The girl was not a great deal younger than herself, and she enjoyed playing fairy godmother to her. Later, when she had her own place, she would give a party for her. She recalled her flame-coloured chiffon dress with a wry smile. Melissa would have appreciated that, but Lord Greenough had taught Toni that it was much more chic to dress quietly.

Mrs Thorne raised no objection to Toni's plans to leave her. She considered her protégée should uphold her new status with an establishment of her own. Nor did she have any qualms about the freedom Toni would thus attain.

'The days of chaperons and duennas are ended,' she remarked. 'You should know your way about by now and if you're going to make a fool of yourself you'll do it whether you're living with me or on your own.'

But Toni had been unable to find anything suitable that was not astronomical in price. Oliver, in whom she had confided, came up with several impossible addresses, studio flats in Chelsea and Soho, which were not only expensive but far too trendy for her taste. She wanted somewhere where she could relax amid restful surroundings, not a mews or an attic amid similar accommodation where the blare of transistors never ceased and long-haired, uncouth-looking students and artists made free with each other's premises. Moreover, he made it plain that he expected to move in with her, and her firm refusal caused a coolness between them.

'You're Victorian,' he scoffed, 'both in your tastes and your morals. The days of repression are over. To fully develop your personality you must take a lover.'

'Perhaps I have one,' she returned.

'Nonsense, little one, you haven't got the glow and ripeness of a woman who loves and is beloved. You're missing so much. If only you'd let me teach you how to live!'

'Your sort of living doesn't appeal to me,' she told him coldly. 'I think you're talking a load of rubbish.'

But she wondered if there was not some truth in what he said. Without love she was only half a woman and though he did not attract her there were other men. If Julian were unobtainable should she not experiment with someone who was? But the thought of other men's embraces nauseated her and she knew she could never bring herself to betray her love ... or hate ... or whatever it was she felt for Julian. Though her primary aim was to mortify him, as he had humiliated her, his hold over her heart and imagination was too deep and long-standing to be easily broken. To cut him out of her thoughts and dreams would be like an amputation.

January was mild that year and *Pygmalion* played to full houses throughout the month, which brought no word at all from Julian. He seemed to have abandoned her even to the extent of forgetting the promised Christmas present, nor did she have any word from Linda. She wondered uneasily if he had taken up with Jessamine again—he had said he must look her up.

Then one morning when Toni was getting ready to go out, Annabel who was at home with a cold came rushing into her bedroom crying:

'Your cousin's here, Toni. He would call when I've got a red nose!'

Since she was piqued by his dilatoriness, Toni wished he had come a few moments later and found her out, when he would have had to console himself with Annabel's red nose. She had already put on her hat and coat, the hat a becoming little fur toque to match her fur coat, but Annabel had betrayed her presence, so she would have to go and greet him. It was a dark day, not actually foggy but dull and unpleasant, necessitating putting the lights on indoors. Julian was standing with his back to the electric fire in the sitting room and Annabel had offered to take his coat, brown suede with a lambswool collar, but he had declined, saying he was not staying long. As Toni came in she had suggested a drink.

'A drop of whisky, it's such a nasty day.'

'Thanks. I find the damp does get to my bones after the African sunshine.'

Toni came forward as Annabel went to obtain the drink.

'Hi, Julian, you're a stranger. You've only just caught me—I was going out. I can only stay a few minutes, I've an appointment.'

She was deliberately unwelcoming, though her heart had lurched at sight of him. He had lost some of his tan during the English winter, but his hair was still the colour of corn, his eyes as brilliantly blue. He gave her a reproachful look.

'That's a pity. I've found a flat for you and I was hoping you could come to see it.'

She was astonished. 'You've found a flat?'

121

'Yes. Wasn't that what you asked me to do?'

Annabel reappeared carrying a tray of drinks.

'Say when,' she bade him, taking the stopper out of the whisky decanter.

Julian's attention was diverted while Toni recovered from her surprise. She had been so sure Julian had forgotten all about her affairs in a press of business at Whiteladies, which was partly what had annoyed her. He turned back to her, lifting his glass.

'Cheers, but won't you join me?'

'No, thank you, I don't drink spirits, at least not in the morning.'

'I will,' Annabel announced, eyeing Julian with obvious appreciation. 'It does my cold good.'

'But how could you find a flat while you've been in Shropshire?' Toni demanded. 'You *have* been at Whiteladies, haven't you?'

'Of course, but there are agents and telephones.' A shadow crossed his face. 'The old man's had another heart attack since Christmas.'

'Oh no!' Toni's pique was forgotten. 'Why wasn't I told?'

'There was nothing you could do, and we didn't want to upset you while you're working so hard. He's got over it, but he has to be very careful from now on. That's why I haven't come to see you sooner.'

'You might have rung me,' she said reproachfully. 'I'm very fond of Uncle Edgar. Zia and I don't communicate very often, but that doesn't mean I don't think a lot about Whiteladies.'

Again she had the feeling of being deliberately excluded, as when her uncle had been ill before, as if she had no place in the family life at Whiteladies, and of course Julian did not accept that she was a member of the Everard clan. That revived her old resentment and the look she gave Julian was hostile. Annabel discreetly withdrew.

'Well, he's all right again now,' Julian told her, ignoring her reproach.

('Until the next attack,' hung in the air between them.)

'I might manage to come down for a weekend,' she said eagerly. 'I'd like to see him.' (Before it was too late.)

'I thought you were too tied up with your play.'

'I could catch a night train on Saturday and return on Monday morning,' she explained.

'You'd exhaust yourself,' he said shortly, and she gained the impression that he did not want her to visit her home, and it was her home while Edgar lived and until it had a new mistress. He went on: 'But to get back to your flat. It's near Regent's Park, an old house that's been converted. Nice position.'

'An old house?' she queried doubtfully.

'So much more spacious than the modern rabbit-hutches. When can you come and see it?'

His manner conveyed repressed eagerness. The place must be something special and there was no reason why she should not go then and there. Her appointment had been a fiction.

'Couldn't you put off your engagement and come now?' he asked persuasively. 'I can't stay long in London.'

Toni realised she was being very ungracious. He must have put himself to a lot of trouble upon her account and at a time when he must have been hard pressed by his father's illness and everything depending upon him, but she had been so taken aback when she had convinced herself that he had forgotten all about her.

'You're acting very nobly since I know you don't like the idea of my living alone,' she remarked.

'No more I do, but I can't stop you, and I would prefer to know you're living in a decent neighbourhood.'

Toni laughed, recalling the mews and near slums that Oliver had advocated. Julian was running true to type. The decayed grandeur of the Regent's Park terraces would appeal to his sense of fitness.

'Thanks very much, I'd love to see it,' she said with more warmth. 'I'll skip my appointment. How do we go? By bus?'

'You look too expensive for a bus,' he observed, appraising her fur coat and not recognising it as only dyed rabbit. 'I've got my car outside. I came up by road.'

'Then let's go,' she suggested.

He drained his glass and put it back on the tray. 'What about Annabel? Would she like to come along?'

'She's off work with a cold,' Toni told him, wondering if he did not want to be alone with her. 'So she can hardly go out. I'll tell her we're off.'

His car drew up in front of a terrace of Georgian houses, of which most had been turned into offices, but a few were still residences. Julian led the way up a flight of steps ending in a pillared portico and through into a tiled hall. The caretaker was on duty, looking up from his cubbyhole by the stairs to nod to Julian. They proceeded up to the first floor, where he produced a key that admitted them to a small vestibule. A blast of warm air greeted them.

'Better take your coat off,' Julian advised, 'the central heating has been turned on.'

Toni slipped off her coat and he hung it up beside his own. Toni glanced at the two garments hanging side by side as they would hang if she and Julian were in residence. To live together had always been her dream and she gave him a sidelong glance, but of course no such idea had ever or ever would occur to him. He was wearing fawn slacks and fawn sweater which toned beautifully with the gold of his hair.

'This is the sitting room,' he said, and threw open the nearest door with a proprietorial air.

It was a high-ceilinged, well-proportioned room and had been newly decorated in cream and gold; moreover it was furnished, the curtains at the two tall windows, the covers of the two armchairs and couch being in a Regency pattern of striped red and gold. The polished table and cabinet she recognised, and the big wall mirror; they had come from Whiteladies. The whole room had the same air of gracious living that had characterised the old house.

'It's lovely, Julian,' she said gratefully, 'but these things ... you said some bits and pieces, but they're good stuff.'

'They could be spared,' he told her. 'We've a lot more junk than we need.'

'Junk!' She ran her fingers along the surface of the polished table.

'Your aunt and uncle consider that as a member of the family you're entitled to some of the loot of generations,' he observed lightly.

She noticed his wording. Linda and Edgar considered her one of the family, but he did not. She wondered if he approved of his parents' generosity.

'And you've done all this ...' she waved her hand, 'without consulting me? I might have been already fixed up.'

'Annabel assured me you were not.'

'So Annabel is in the conspiracy too?' He must have contacted her friend in the evening, when he knew she herself would be out.

He looked hurt. 'Don't you like it? I meant it to be a surprise for you, my belated Christmas present.'

'It's charming,' she said slowly. 'But you were taking a chance, you know.'

'Was I?' He smiled confidently. 'I think I know your tastes. Come and see the bedroom.'

This was connected with the sitting room by a door. In the old days they had been the rooms for entertaining. It was another spacious room done in shades of blue, with a new divan bed and a dressing table she again recognised. A large piece of furniture with a well between two tiers of small drawers and a large mirror.

'Of course you can in time replace the furniture with something more modern if you so wish,' Julian told her. 'But this will do for a start.'

'I would never want to replace anything,' she cried impulsively. 'How you must have worked over it, and I thought you'd forgotten.'

'Oh, the movers and the decorators did the work. I only made the arrangements,' he said carelessly.

'But however did you find it? Places like this aren't easy to come by.'

'Jessamine's father, Mr Boycott, deals in property. He got it for me . . . I mean you.'

Toni's enthusiasm was damped.

'How is Jessamine?' she asked flatly.

'Very well, I believe. I haven't seen her yet. She's spending the winter in America.'

Toni drew a long breath. When Julian had mentioned Mr Boycott she had been on the verge of refusing the accommodation, saying she could not possibly live there, but common sense prevailed. She would never find anything better, even though the connection with the Boycotts was unpalatable.

'Does Mr Boycott own the house?' she inquired.

'Oh no, it belongs to a syndicate. I've settled all the formalities for you, Toni, it only requires your signature to some papers, and ... er... if the rent gets too much for you, let us know and we'll help. Mother was most emphatic that you were to be properly housed. She seemed to have an idea that you might land up in a verminous attic, imagining it was what was expected of an actress.'

'I'm really most grateful,' Toni assured him, glad that she would have no contact with the Boycotts, 'and at present I'm earning good money.' She was a little chagrined that he seemed so anxious to attribute more credit to Linda than to himself, as if his efforts on her behalf had had to be prompted by his mother. His wariness tempered the quality of her gratitude.

Julian showed her the rest of the flat, kitchen, bathroom and small second bedroom, obviously conversions. The last would do well for Ellen.

'You can move in at once,' he told her when they had regained the sitting room. The long mirror reflected Toni's slight figure in white sweater and fawn skirt, a striped overblouse in black, white and fawn covering the sweater. Julian's eyes were on it as he went on: 'It's the right setting for you, Toni.'

'Oliver won't approve, he's all for the avant-garde,' Toni remarked idly.

Julian frowned at the mention of the actor. 'He's quite wrong. You're not a modern type. You put me in mind of a Florentine painting.'

'Thanks.' But she was not pleased. He was seeing her as all Italian.

'I suppose it's inevitable he'll visit you here?' he asked.

Because his observation about being Florentine had needled her, she returned provocatively:

'Of course. You can't expect me to live like a nun.'

A look of anxiety crossed his face. 'Toni, you will behave yourself?'

'I've no intention of going to bed with him,' she retorted flippantly. 'For one thing, he's much too old.' She moved away from the mirror towards the door. 'But it's most unfashionable to be a virgin.'

In a couple of strides he reached her, gripping her waist and swinging her round to face him.

'Toni, I've done my best to please you and if you've any gratitude you'll promise me to be a good girl.' The words were simple, almost banal, but his eyes held the same glitter as when he had seen her in Oliver's arms and his fingers dug remorselessly into the flesh of her waist. It flashed into her mind that whatever he felt towards her, he hated to think of her being possessed by another man.

'You mean, to remain immaculate?' She looked up into his lean face with an imp of devilment dancing in her black eyes. 'That's difficult these days, Julian. Oliver considers I need initiating into being a woman ... a real woman.' She laughed wickedly. 'Perhaps you would prefer to initiate me yourself.'

The feel of her slim body between his hands was exciting him, as she well knew. He shifted his grip from her waist to enclose her and held her close against himself, his breathing hurried.

'If any bounder dares to seduce you ...' he threatened.

'That isn't what I asked,' she returned. 'It's bound to happen one day, Julian. You know very well I'm not an icicle. The question is ... who?'

'There's only one thing for it,' he said between clenched teeth. 'I'll have to marry you.'

He had said it, words she had longed to hear, but now

they had come much too late. Between them was the barrier of her bitter resentment and humiliation. Nor did she believe he really meant what he had said. Upon reflection he would try to pass it off as a joke, when he remembered what he believed her to be.

She put her hands against his chest and tried to push him away.

'I don't want a keeper, Julian, I want to be free.'

'Not your keeper, Toni, your lover and husband,' he said ardently, and overcoming her halfhearted resistance he tightened his hold of her and sought her mouth. 'Oh, Toni,' he murmured between his kisses, 'I've fought against you for so long, but it's no use.'

The nameless something that had always been between them erupted in a fiery flood. Julian had thrown aside restraint, his scruples were forgotten. Toni's passion surged up in a great wave of rapture to meet his. She clung to him, giving back kiss for kiss. He picked her up and carrying her over to the wide couch, laid her down upon it, stretching himself beside her. His hand pulled at the neck of her sweater, dragging it down so that his lips could find the soft skin at the base of her throat. His weight pressed her into the yielding surface of the couch.

'My little Italian seductress,' he murmured.

Italian again! She was not Italian, she was British, and Lewis Everard's daughter. She had deliberately provoked him, hoping to arouse him, and her body had responded to the first urgency of his passion, but now her mind took over. It was not her intention to allow herself to submit to him wholly. She suspected that now he had mentioned marriage he thought he could do with her what he pleased. The little Italian nobody would not be particular since he believed her mother had been wanton. Later, when his madness had passed, he would bitterly regret his rash proposal, for Maria's child was not worthy to be mistress of Whiteladies. He would keep his word, for his code would not permit him to break it, but his reluctance would be apparent, for hadn't he always sought to resist her, and that would be painful to her.

She had brought him to the point where her rejection would hurt him, and that was to be her revenge. She would not weaken now with success in sight, though his kisses had been sweet and satisfying. Her limp body stiffened and she turned her head away to avoid his seeking lips. Surprised, he slackened his hold. Though he was far stronger than she, she was supple as an eel and she contrived to slide away from him. She walked over to the mirror, striving to subdue the turmoil in her blood, for during the next act in their drama she needed to be cool.

Julian turned over on to his back and lay watching her with eyes of flickering flame.

'Come back,' he commanded.

The imperious order thrilled her as male dominance always did, and she had to resist an urge to obey him. Reaching for her handbag, and taking out the comb it contained, she slowly and carefully tidied her hair and smoothed her rumpled clothing. In the mirror she could see his recumbent form and saw Julian's expression change to a faint puzzlement. He had been so sure of her surrender. That stung her. She had always been the one to make the first advances, and now he had condescended to reciprocate he was unable to account for her withdrawal.

Julian swung his legs off the couch and sat up, the flame dying out of his eyes, gazing at her unresponsive back half apologetically. Her silence indicated that he had offended her. Smoothing his ruffled hair with one hand, he said wryly:

'I'm afraid that was a bit of a rough-house, but you drive a man mad, my Toni.'

She could watch him in the mirror, but it was so angled that he could not see her face. So he was going to blame her for his lack of self-control and he could no longer excuse her on the plea of not knowing what she was doing, now she was adult.

'Don't you think my technique has improved?' she asked wickedly.

His lips tightened to a thin line as he stared at her straight back.

'It's more than ever evident that you need protecting,' he said acidly. Then he smiled. 'I'm offering my services.'

'To guard my innocence?' she demanded truculently.

'Turn round, Toni, I'm tired of addressing your back. Yes, my child, just that. Do you accept my offer?'

Toni swung round with a scornful gleam in her eyes.

'If I want a protector I can find a richer man than you, Julian.'

He looked startled. 'Really, Toni, I didn't mean that! I'm asking you to marry me.'

Toni drew a deep breath. This was the moment for which she had schemed, the salve for her wounded pride. She had rehearsed many times what she would say if it ever came and the words she uttered were like the well conned lines of a play.

'If I decide to marry I'd prefer a younger man than you. You're seventeen years older than I, middle-aged in fact. You might just be my father.'

If only he had spoken of love she might have relented, but his talk of protection riled her. For one thing, it was so old-fashioned. There had been a time when he had held her whole heart, he was the only being she did love, and he had brushed her off as being a foolish child. She knew his proposal had been wrung from him by the force of his desire and when he had time to think he would scorn himself for yielding to it.

'Youth turns to youth,' she continued lightly. 'I've plenty of younger men lined up to choose from, if I want one. I've considered taking a lover, just to see what it was like.'

She saw his face become hard and cold, his eyes like blue ice, and he looked at her as if he had never seen her before.

'So this is what the stage has done for you!' he exclaimed. 'You used to be so sweet and innocent.'

'I don't think I was ever that,' she objected. 'Naïve and silly perhaps, but as you suggest, I've learned a few things since I've been in London.' An edge of bitterness crept into her voice. 'You always told me I'd grow out of my schoolgirl infatuation for you.'

'It didn't seem you had just now.'

'Oh, that!' She dismissed the incident with a wave of her hand. 'I was experimenting. I wanted to see how far you'd go. Really, Julian, you should be ashamed of yourself, a man of your age—but I suppose you were starved of women in Africa.'

He sprang to his feet and took a couple of strides towards her with such a look of fury on his face that she thought he was going to strike her. Some primitive emotion stirred deep within her in response to the violence he threatened to unleash. If he had taken her then she would have surrendered utterly, but he mastered himself; he had long since learned to control a nature as passionate as her own. Turning away from her, he said coldly:

'That's enough, Toni. I get the message. The subject

is closed. If you've seen all you wish to see we'd better go. There's your key.' He threw it down on the table. 'I'll drop you at Mrs Thorne's and then I must be on my way. I want to be back at Whiteladies tonight and it's a long trek.'

Mechanically she picked up the key and moved towards the door. Already her resentment was fading, to be replaced by a vague regret. In silence they resumed their coats and made their way down to the car. Neither spoke as Julian drove her back to Bayswater. Toni's exultation over her victory died, for her revenge had lost its savour. Whatever had motivated her, love, hate, the desire for retaliation, Julian had been, was still and always would be the dominant influence in her life, and now she had alienated him entirely. One glance at his set profile assured her that he would never forgive the rebuff she had given him.

He drew up outside the block of flats where the Thornes lived, and she made an effort to thank him for what he had done on her behalf, but her words sounded stilted and formal.

'Think nothing of it,' he told her. 'Most of it was Mother's doing.'

'I'll write to her.'

'Yes, she'll appreciate that.' He looked at her with a slight wistfulness. 'If you're really grateful, be good. We'd hate to think we'd been instrumental in giving you greater freedom to your harm.'

She smiled wryly, all resentment quenched.

'Present-day youth talks a lot of hot air,' she admitted. 'We like to sound daring and with it, but most of us are chary of putting what we advocate into practice.'

'I hope that's so in your case,' he said stiffly.

'Okay, schoolmaster, I'm really very circumspect.'

Except where he was concerned.

'No more ... er ... experimenting?' he asked with a wry smile.

'I didn't find it so enjoyable I want to repeat it,' she declared, perversely adding to the wound she had already dealt, and saw him wince. Instantly her heart misgave her, but could he really believe she found his kisses unpleasant? How very, very far he was from understanding her! 'Love affairs aren't really much in my line,' she went on. 'I intend to dedicate myself to my profession.'

The last sentence sounded a little pretentious and he looked faintly amused.

'I'm glad to hear it.' He glanced at his watch. 'I really must say goodbye. As I said, I've a long way to go.'

She opened the car door. 'Goodbye, Julian. Remember me to Zia and Uncle Edgar, and I do hope he keeps well.'

Formal words again. She stepped out of the car on to the pavement and closed the door. Julian lifted a hand in valediction, put the car in gear and glided away. Toni stood watching it disappear into the winter murk with an ache in her heart. She had played her great repudiation scene according to plan, and somehow it had badly misfired.

CHAPTER EIGHT

FAR from feeling the satisfaction she had anticipated from her rejection of Julian, Toni was overwhelmed by shame and regret. Though she had succeeded beyond her wildest hopes by wringing a proposal of marriage from him, her conduct had been that of a first-class bitch. When she had enlisted his aid in finding a home for her her object had been to maintain contact with him, and in this she had failed, because he had found accommodation for her without consulting her with the intention of giving her a pleasant surprise. He had given considerable time and trouble to his quest at a time when he was busy with his own concerns and anxious about his father. She had repaid him by tempting him beyond his powers of resistance, for every glance and word she had bestowed upon him in the flat had been deliberately provocative and inciting, and then she had spurned him. In vain she told herself that her behaviour had been what he would expect from her mother's daughter, and recalling the slur he had put upon Maria's memory, sought to stir up the embers of her once burning resentment. It was no use, those ashes would yield no flame. Maria had been dead a long time and even if she were alive would neither understand nor appreciate her child's misguided loyalty.

What Toni was forced to realise was that her love had never died and now she had finally driven Julian away, she was left with a sense of a great emptiness. First her love and then her hate had filled her horizon with purpose. Now there was nothing.

She still had her profession and for the first time she gave it her full concentration, striving to fill the void that Julian had left.

She had been engaged to play in a costume drama which was to follow *Pygmalion*, a play about the Siddons family, her part being that of the flighty Maria, who was determined to annex her sister's lover, Tom Lawrence. Her most telling scene was where on her deathbed she makes the reluctant Sally promise never to make it up with Tom, who for a brief space of time had deserted the elder for the younger sister, being beguiled by Maria during one of Sally's illnesses. Both girls suffered from the consumptive scourge prevalent at that period. Maria had been a spoilt young minx, and the part might have been tailored for Toni. She found when it went into rehearsal, as it did while *Pygmalion* was still running, that she could find release for her pent-up emotions in the hysterical tantrums of the Siddons girl.

Meanwhile she moved with some reluctance into her new flat, for it was so impregnated by her last dreadful scene with Julian that she shrank from occupying it. But that was a foolishness she had to overcome, for she must go somewhere, and in time the furniture he had chosen for her from Whiteladies gave her solace. It had brought with it something of the serene atmosphere of the old house that had been the only home she had known since she left Italy.

Though delighted to look after her, Ellen was critical of the flat. Its elegant austerity repelled her. A famous actress should have more opulent surroundings. She was to continue with her work at the theatre in the evenings, but during the day she would tend to Toni's comfort. One thing puzzled her. It was quite in keeping with theatre traditions for an actress to be provided with an establishment by a wealthy admirer, but no male visitor came to see Toni and claim his due. That seemed to Ellen's simple mind to be all wrong. Her beautiful mistress needed a man. Once, greatly daring, she approached the subject.

'You're always alone, ma'am. It's not good for a young lady to be alone.'

'I'm not alone, Ellen, I have you,' Toni pointed out. 'My work takes all my energy and I want to be quiet when I'm at home.'

'But the gentleman who rent this flat ... does he not come?'

Toni turned away to hide the pain she feared she might betray.

'He's busy with his own affairs. He ... he's a relation, that's why he helped me to find it. Now I'm settled he has other things to do. He lives a long way away in the country.'

Ellen was far from satisfied. She was sure her young mistress was pining for the elusive 'relation'. They must have quarrelled, and being a devout Christian she added to her nightly prayers a petition that they might be reconciled.

Annabel too did not approve of the decor of Toni's new abode.

'It looks like something out of Jane Austen,' she complained. 'I really think Julian might have found you something more with it. The furnishings look as if they came out of the Ark. When I have a flat, as I hope to one day, I'll have a black ceiling and walls in different colours with a lot of big pouffes and squashy cushions. You haven't got a cocktail bar nor a radiogram—whatever will you do when you throw a party?'

'I'm not intending to give any parties,' Toni told her. She had thought of inviting the members of the cast for a Sunday evening, but that would have to include Oliver, who might be difficult to dislodge. 'I find my part a little exhausting, especially now we're rehearsing during the daytime. I like peace and quiet when I'm at home.'

'You might be a hundred,' Annabel grumbled, who had hoped for wild orgies now Toni was on her own.

'Sometimes I feel it,' Toni sighed, feeling she had packed too much emotion into her few years. 'I like the atmosphere of this place and ...' She hesitated. 'Julian said it was me.'

Annabel considered this statement.

'Perhaps he'd got something,' she admitted. 'There is something period about you, Toni. You don't look modern, you've got a classic face.'

'I expect you'd find plenty like me in Italy,' Toni remarked.

'I suppose that's it. Was your mother very beautiful?'

'She grew fat and blowsy,' Toni said harshly. 'But my father was an Everard and as blond as Julian.' She lifted her head defiantly. She would maintain that Lewis was her sire until her dying day.

'How odd.' Annabel had no idea that she was treading upon dangerous ground and her comments might be wounding. 'You're not the least like the rest of your family, are you?'

'That has been said before,' Toni observed acidly, and changed the subject.

With rehearsals for *The Siddons Story* during the daytime and *Pygmalion* at night Toni's days were full, and she was glad of that for it left little time for repining. She rang Whiteladies several times to inquire about her great-uncle. Linda said he seemed to have recovered but was very frail. She promised to let Toni know if there were any change. Hungering for the sound of his voice, Toni had hoped Julian might answer her call, but her aunt said he was rarely indoors; he was occupied with the spring cultivation.

'He has no need to work so hard,' his mother declared. 'It seems that having at last taken to farming he can't do enough.'

This news gave Toni a faint satisfaction. It would appear that Julian too had a need to absorb himself in work, but was it because of her or to combat his yearnings for a more adventurous life? It was more likely to be the latter.

Oliver had at last given up his siege of her. He would

not be in her next play, as he was going to America. He called her several unpleasant names which she knew meant a girl who aroused expectations she did not intend to satisfy, which in his case was quite unjust. She had never done more than flirt mildly with him, and she had always given him to understand she would go no further.

'You're peeved because you've found you aren't irresistible,' she told him.

'I would be if you were a real woman. Your trouble is that you've a lump of ice where your heart should be.'

'Come off it, Oliver, just because it won't melt for you . . .'

He had remembered something.

'You mean it did melt for that guy who turned up on our opening night? I hear he's set you up in that nice little pad you've got where you'll never ask me in. But he's never there—Ellen admits that. He couldn't blame you if you console yourself.'

This conversation took place when Toni encountered him on her way to the stage door. Other people including stage hands kept passing them and he did not lower his voice. Toni was furious.

'So you question my dresser about my private life!' she accused him in a low angry voice. 'You're despicable, Oliver. You're the last person I'd ever come to for consolation!'

She swept past him, wondering how many people had overheard his remarks. Not that she cared if it were surmised that Julian was keeping her, but the rub was that he was not. She never saw him.

Then one night during the last week of the run, when Toni was changing ready to go home, Ellen brought her a message. A Miss Boycott was asking to see her.

'In a minute,' Toni said, pulling on her dress and

139

turning so Ellen could pull up the zip. She hastily powdered her face and ran a comb through her hair. 'All right, show her in.'

She was aware of a sudden premonition. What had Jessamine come to tell her? Nothing she wanted to hear, she was sure.

The years that had elapsed since their last meeting had made little alteration to Jessamine Boycott. She had lost a little of her bloom, was thinner and dressed with more style. Toni calculated that she must be nearing thirty. She had evidently been in front, for she wore a semi-evening dress and a fur coat. Toni's simple dress with its pleated skirt made her look young and girlish beside the elder woman's assurance. She signed to Ellen to leave them and the dresser slipped out into the passage.

'I wanted to say how much I enjoyed your performance,' Jessamine said conventionally.

'Thank you.' Toni's expression was guarded. 'Won't you sit down?' She indicated the couch upon which she rested between performances on matinee days.

Jessamine looked at it rather as if she expected it to be verminous, and perched herself on the edge of it. Toni sat down on the chair in front of the mirror and surveyed her visitor.

'You've certainly made good,' Jessamine went on. 'Surprising, when I remember what a little savage you were when I met you in Shropshire.'

'I suppose I did seem so to you,' Toni admitted, her eyes glinting. Both were remembering the flame-coloured dress. How like Jessamine to conceal a claw when she gave a pat on the back! 'But my savagery, as you call it, was merely excess of temperament. I learned to control it, like the rest of my emotional power which is necessary to my art.'

'Is that what you call it?' Jessamine asked with a sneer. 'Thank goodness I've no artistic temperament. It must be most uncomfortable, driving one to do such unpredictable things.' Toni wondered how much Julian had told her about her subsequent behaviour on that memorable night when she had overheard their conversation. It was all so long ago, but Jessamine would not forget anything that was to her detriment. Miss Boycott settled herself more comfortably on the couch and announced complacently:

'I've been asked to stay again at Whiteladies. Such a beautiful old house, isn't it? I'm delighted to be visiting it again. Incidentally, I understand it's difficult for you to leave London, so if you've any messages, I'd be glad to take them.'

'Thank you, but I can always ring up if I've anything to tell my family.' Toni emphasised the last two words and Jessamine raised her arched brows, while a chill crept round her heart. If Jessamine were going to stay at Whiteladies it could mean only one thing. Julian had asked his mother to invite her so that they could resume their former relationship, and that was what Jessamine meant to convey to her. She had expected it, but the confirmation of her fears hit her all the same.

'Yes, of course,' Jessamine assented. 'I'm so sorry to hear that poor Mr Everard has been so poorly. I gather it's only a matter of time?' She looked at Toni interrogatively.

Noticing the avaricious gleam in the grey-blue eyes, Toni felt a hot rush of anger. Jessamine was not sorry at all, she was relishing the assumption that Julian would soon be master of Whiteladies, if the taxes left him master of anything. Julian had asked her down to clinch their engagement, for when he assumed his new duties he would need a wife, as had been so often pointed out. Linda would be jubilant. She had always favoured this match, and Jessamine could not resist coming to crow over Toni before she left, who she had suspected had been a spoke in her wheel.

Mastering her rage, Toni remarked with apparent calm:

'They do say creaking gates hang the longest, and I hope Uncle Edgar will be with us for a long while yet.'

She longed to puncture her visitor's self-satisfaction.

'Of course I hope so too, but you never know with a heart condition.' Jessamine shrugged her shoulders. 'But it must be a great relief to them all that you're doing so well for yourself and they need feel no further responsibility for you.'

Jessamine had predicted that Toni would eventually bring shame to the proud Everards who had fostered her. She had not done that, though Jessamine's expression, belying her words, rather suggested that they would not appreciate being connected with the stage.

'Yes, it must be a great relief to all concerned,' Toni returned, well knowing that Jessamine was thankful to have her out of the way. 'But I still regard White-ladies as my home.'

Again the arched brows rose.

'It can't be that when Julian marries,' Jessamine purred. 'Though of course you'd always be welcome as a visitor, I suppose. His wife could hardly object to that.'

'Wouldn't she?' Toni grinned impishly. 'Don't worry, Jessamine, I'll not strain anyone's hospitality. I'd have no inducement to return if my uncle and aunt aren't there, and I have got a place of my own now.'

'Which I understand is furnished with some rather good pieces from Whiteladies, presumably on loan.'

Toni felt another rush of anger. Did Jessamine begrudge her what Julian had given her? She wondered how she could have known, and then remembered that Julian had consulted Mr Boycott about finding the flat. He must have told him how he proposed to furnish it.

'Julian arranged everything for me,' Toni said coldly, 'He didn't say anything about loans.'

'No, he's inclined to be careless where his family is concerned,' Jessamine observed. 'So many people are, then when ... er ... anything happens there are disputes about ownership. But I expect Mr Everard will have kept an inventory and tied up all the loose ends. He's very businesslike.' She laughed affectedly. 'It doesn't do to leave things to chance, does it?'

'Uncle Edgar won't forget me,' Toni assured her, not because she expected anything from her great-uncle or wanted it, but to annoy Jessamine.

The grey-blue eyes narrowed maliciously.

'He doesn't owe you anything ... not under the circumstances,' Jessamine pointed out. It was a cruel thing to say, revealing, if Toni had not known already, that Julian had made her his confidant. Jessamine was not naturally vindictive, but she had been deeply chagrined when Julian had fled to Africa instead of proposing as she had expected. Intuitively she suspected that Toni was in some way connected with his disappearance. The girl was far too good-looking and embarrassingly direct. A natural coquette, Jessamine had assured herself, and such women learned seduction in the cradle. Since Julian had escaped from her toils she had turned her attention to his father to secure her pickings. Thus Jessamine justified herself to excuse her jealousy.

Toni returned her glance with a hard cool stare. She was being told that she could expect nothing from a family that was not her kin, but not by the quiver of an eyelash did she betray that the shaft had gone home. She had no expectations, though she would like to keep her furniture in memory of Whiteladies, nor did she believe that anyone except Jessamine would grudge it to her. She wondered if Julian had ever hinted to his father that she might not in reality be his great-niece. She did not think so, for that would touch his family pride which his son would not wish to wound.

'It has nothing to do with you ... yet,' she said icily. 'And I'm sure Uncle Edgar is going to live for a long while. Even if he has got a weak heart, he's no great age.' She stood up and reached for her coat. 'Now I must ask you to excuse me, my car will be waiting for me.'

Toni had not yet acquired a vehicle of her own, but she hired one to take her home each night.

Jessamine rose to her feet.

'Goodbye, Antonia, and here's wishing you continued good luck. I hear the next venture is *The Siddons Story*, and you're to play the bitchy sister, Maria. I'm sure you'll be excellent.'

Toni grinned impishly.

'I should be, shouldn't I? I've had plenty of practice.'

'You've said it, not I,' Jessamine returned.

'No, but you implied it. Goodnight, Miss Boycott.'

But when Jessamine had gone a heavy weight of depression descended upon Toni. It would be easier to bear her heartache if Julian had taken up with someone other than Jessamine, who she could not believe would make him happy. As many women did before marriage, Jessamine had only shown him her best side and he could have no notion of her true character.

The Siddons Story was booked for another theatre, so Toni was to vacate her dressing room on the last night of *Pygmalion*. The rest of the cast were going on to a party for which Toni had little inclination, for after a matinee followed by the evening show with its speeches and curtain calls, she would be exhausted. She had been presented with enough flowers to stock a greenhouse, and she arranged that they should be sent to the nearest hospital. Leaving Ellen to clear up, she left the theatre with a nostalgic feeling, for it had been the scene of her first triumph and there Julian had come to her upon his return. She had had no close friend in front that night. Even the faithful Annabel had had another engagement, and Oliver was so incensed he would not speak to her. She made a great effort to appear gay and bright when she reached the party, and left as soon as she could. Arrived at the flat, she found that Ellen had brought back a bunch of red roses which she had put in a vase in the sitting room.

'I thought you wouldn't want to part with those, ma'am,' she explained with a sly look. 'They're from Mr Julian Everard.'

She triumphantly produced his card, and as she took it, Toni felt a lump rise in her throat. So in spite of everything Julian had remembered it was her last night! The card was inscribed:

'Only the first, I hope, of many great successes. Yours, Julian.'

Suddenly she had a desperate longing for his presence as friend and supporter. Why had she been such a fool as to throw away her happiness to avenge a supposed slight? Julian might have repented of his rash proposal, but he would not have gone back upon his word, and surely she could have made him happier than that supercilious young woman who had superceded her?

She became aware that Ellen was watching her with compassionate dark eyes. She had long suspected an absent lover for whom her mistress was hankering, the man with the sunlight in his hair who had appeared upon her opening night and never since. She had seen how Toni's face had lit up when she mentioned whom the roses were from.

'Now surely he will come,' she said.

'Who?'

'Your lover, ma'am.'

Toni shook her head. 'I have no lover, and I'm longing for my bed.'

'It is not good to sleep alone,' Ellen told her. 'If not that one, there are others. You've many admirers, ma'am.'

'There's only one for me, and he doesn't want me,' Toni informed her. She had decided Julian had sent the flowers as a valedictory offering, the end of her first stage appearance which marked the finale of their association, for Jessamine was going to Whiteladies to become engaged to him.

Since a stage was unavailable for the first rehearsals, *The Siddons Story* was banished to dingy rehearsal rooms which as spring advanced seemed hot and airless contrasted with the freshness outside. The costumes would be in the Empire style, long high-waisted garments that clung to the figure in silks and muslins, or rather substitute materials, for who had heard of muslin nowadays? Toni was shown sketches of the designs for her dresses and reproductions of drawings of both sisters attributed to Lawrence, who had portrayed the whole family. She saw she was not unlike Maria with her dark curls and fine features. She had more sympathy for her than the virtuous Sally, even though she was deceitful. She thought she might have made a better fight for her love. Her parents had opposed Sally's engagement to Tom, one reason given being her youth. That plea had always exasperated Toni. Adults were always so sure they knew best, but what right had they to judge? Their hearts were not being broken by enforced separation.

To please Ellen she invited Melissa and her boyfriend to come to supper one evening, now her nights were free. He was a good-looking young fellow, copper-coloured with long curling dark hair and amorous eyes, a little older than Ellen's daughter. At first they were shy and awkward, awestruck by their surroundings and the presence of a genuine actress, unable to do more than meekly answer her polite questions. But under the influence of Ellen's excellent cooking and a bottle of wine, they thawed. The boy, Roddy, had brought his guitar with him and entertained them afterwards with tropical songs and rhythms that set their feet tapping. Excited by the music, Toni sprang up and began to dance, Melissa joined her and they twisted and stamped with youthful exuberance until, exhausted, they both flopped into easy chairs.

'I'd never have thought it!' Melissa exclaimed.

'Thought what?' Toni asked.

'You, miss, so calm and dignified and . . . and famous.' She giggled. 'You didn't half let your hair down!'

It was disarranged by her dancing, a tangled mass about her shoulders.

'But I'm young too,' Toni said, and suddenly sobered. She never had been really young and lighthearted like her two companions, who were laughing and nudging each other like a couple of puppies, Roddy having moved to share Melissa's chair. As a result of the earthquake she had been precipitated into a new world with too many adjustments to make and her obsessive love for Julian had caused her to strive to reach up to him instead of joining in the frolics of her age group. Not that the girls at Greystones had been frolicsome, they were too well disciplined, but even so she had thought

147

they were silly except for Annabel. The consequence was that she had ripened too early, losing her spring-time.

'Now you two behave,' Ellen admonished the couple, interpreting Toni's serious expression as disapproval.

'Let them alone, they're enjoying themselves,' Toni said, smiling. She threw off her introspective mood. 'Come on, Roddy, another tune, something lively.'

Roddy disengaged himself from Melissa and twanged his guitar.

Later they found some light music, Viennese waltzes, on the television set—Toni had installed that modern amenity—and Roddy smooched round the room cheek to cheek with his girl-friend.

'Now give Miss Alderly a turn,' Ellen commanded.

Roddy looked doubtfully at Toni.

'I don't bite,' she said, laughing.

'Go on,' Melissa urged.

Roddy's face broke into an audacious grin, and he took Toni in his arms. She was immediately conscious of his young virility, and his bashfulness vanished as he realised she was young and feminine. They moved in perfect unison over the floor, Toni surrendering herself to the sensuous tune. The boy was, she supposed, about her own age, but she was a century older in experience, except of the elementary things, love and its fulfilment. Then she caught sight of Melissa's face, darkened by anxious jealousy. Roddy was showing too great an appreciation of his new partner. She broke away from him with a laugh.

'Thank you very much, that was nice, but I mustn't monopolise you.'

He went slightly reluctantly back to Melissa.

It was after midnight when the young couple de-parted. Toni asked Ellen anxiously:

'Will they be all right?'

The woman shrugged her shoulders.

'Guess so, ma'am, they're often out late. Can't tell young folk nothing these days.'

'I suppose not.' Toni wondered how Melissa would have fitted into Greystones; the child would not have been very amenable to Miss Selby's teaching on decorum. She herself had submitted to make herself worthy to consort with Julian, and much good that had done her. She would have been happier in a slum with someone like Roddy to play the guitar for her. Perhaps she was not an Everard after all.

Pygmalion had been over for a fortnight and Toni wondered if Jessamine had gone to Whiteladies. She had had no word from there until returning from rehearsal on a lovely day in May, Ellen met her with the information that Mrs Everard had rung up and requested that Miss Alderly would ring her back as soon as she came in. Toni looked at the instrument rather as if it were a snake, her first thought being that Julian must have fulfilled his mother's hopes at last and Linda was wanting to proclaim the good news.

'Shall I get the number for you?' Ellen asked, scenting an emergency and wanting to be helpful.

'No, thanks, I'll do it,' Toni said, tempted not to ring at all. But it might not be Julian's engagement Linda wanted to communicate, it might be that Uncle Edgar was ill again. She had promised to let her know if he had another attack, so she dared not ignore Linda's request.

He had. He was in a hospital's intensive care ward and he wanted to see Toni if she could possibly come down to Shropshire.

'It's urgent,' Linda told her, 'or else I wouldn't have called you. Come if you can, you mayn't have another

149

chance ...' Her voice trailed away, betraying her intense anxiety, though she had spoken with calm self-control. Toni declared that she would come down next day even if it meant jeopardising her part. She would have left that night, but she would have to get in touch with the management to procure leave of absence if possible, and if there were a night train it would be very slow.

In her concern for her uncle she forgot to inquire if Jessamine were at Whiteladies.

Toni arrived at Shrewsbury early the following afternoon. She had not been sacked, though her director was far from pleased by her departure, but a dying relative was an excuse he could not very well override, and Antonia Alderly had become a draw the company would be unwilling to lose. It was not as if the play was actually in performance.

Julian met her at the station, and her heart leaped at the sight of him, so dear and so familiar. He told her his father had rallied a little but was still on the danger list. He was very quiet and grave. He thanked her for coming and said he hoped it had not made difficulties for her, at which Toni smiled.

'I said if they wouldn't release me I'd walk out, and that would have made difficulties for them,' she told him.

She had not met Julian since the morning in her flat, but their mutual anxiety about his father precluded any constraint. He talked quite naturally about Edgar and what was happening on the estate as if there had never been any turgid scene between them. It was not until half the distance was traversed that Toni asked the question she was burning to put.

'Is Jessamine Boycott staying with you?'

'Jess?' He looked surprised. 'Oh yes, she did write

and ask Mother if we could put her up for a few days. She's doing some articles upon historic buildings, apparently—she's taken up writing, you know—and there are several around here, including the Feathers at Ludlow, but of course now Dad's had this attack, we've had to put her off.'

Which was not at all what Jessamine had said, and Toni's spirits rose, until remembering why she had come, she repressed her elation.

Linda greeted her affectionately, remarking that she looked tired.

'I expect you miss the country air, being in London,' she said. 'Personally I'd hate to have to live there.'

After tea she drove her niece to the hospital, saying Julian would come later. Edgar was only allowed short visits by one person at a time.

Toni was shocked when she saw him, propped up against his pillows to ease his breathing. His face was the colour of parchment and he looked so frail that a puff of wind would blow him away. He smiled when he saw her.

'So glad you've come ... always very fond of you, Toni. Well, I guess this is the end of the road for me.'

'You mustn't say that, Uncle,' she exclaimed vehemently. 'You'll get over this attack. You did before.'

He slightly moved his head in negation.

'Glad to go ... so tired. Only you and Julian left, Toni. Last of the Everards.'

Toni swallowed. 'Julian will marry ... have children ...'

He roused himself to say:

'Keep him in England, Toni ... only you can do it. He'll stay for you.'

He closed his eyes and relaxed against his pillows.

Why did he say that? Toni wondered. Did he, now he

151

was so ill, see that to which they had all been so blind? But it was beyond her power to influence Julian now. She had driven him from her.

A nurse appeared and beckoned to her. Toni bent down and kissed her uncle's wasted cheek.

'Goodnight, Uncle Edgar.'

'Goodbye.' It was a mere whisper. 'So proud of you, Toni.'

She was not proud of herself. Thank God he did not know how she had treated Julian. She looked back when she reached the door at the still figure on the bed, and she knew then that she would not see him again.

Edgar Everard died that night. Julian and his wife were with him until the end. Toni, alone at Whiteladies, knew what news they would have for her when they returned at first light. A new day full of fresh problems had dawned for them, but Edgar's sun had set.

CHAPTER NINE

LINDA accepted her husband's death with quiet resignation, for she had been expecting it. Toni marvelled at her self-control, for though he had left a great gap in her life, she gave no outward demonstration of grief but turned her practical mind towards her future plans. In similar circumstances Toni was sure she would herself have been prostrate with grief—not that Linda was heartless, but her reserved nature shrank from any display of emotion, which in her childhood Toni had mistaken for coldness and indifference.

Toni telephoned her manager and said she must stay in Shropshire for the funeral. She was informed that the production had been halted, as the actress playing Mrs Siddons had been rushed into hospital with appendicitis, and the actor cast for Tom Lawrence had broken his ankle. It seemed there was a jinx on the play, as there were other snags, and it was possible it would have to be abandoned.

Though it would mean a financial loss to her, Toni felt only relief; the woes of the Siddons family were too remote to interest her now. All she wanted to do was to stay on at Whiteladies and comfort her aunt and cousin if they would let her, but Julian was as withdrawn as his mother. The house was enfolded in that muted atmosphere that always attends a death and he was occupied with all the necessary arrangements for the funeral besides keeping the farm running. He was rarely in for meals and became immersed in paper work during the evenings. It was then Linda did turn to Toni for comfort, saying how glad she was the girl was there to assuage her loneliness.

The day before the funeral, Toni's agent rang her up to tell her she was to be auditioned for the part of Lady Caroline Lamb in a television series about Lord Byron. She arranged to come up to London for a day and a night and advised Ellen accordingly. It was a relief to have a prospect of work now the Siddons play was in abeyance, but she did not much care for the role. She seemed condemned to play bitchy parts, she reflected wryly.

Most of the county attended Edgar Everard's obsequies, for he had been well known among what was left of the gentry. All spoke of him with respect and regret. They were for the most part a collection of old has-beens, retired Service men, colonels and commanders, dispossessed squires and yeomen, few of whom were still in possession of their estates. Over all hung the unspoken question, would Julian Everard be able to carry on?'

The Boycotts sent a wreath and condolences. To Toni's relief it was not suggested that Jessamine should attend the funeral. It was taken for granted that the distance from London was too great, nor did Julian appear to consider she was a sufficiently intimate friend to be asked. Toni recalled that according to him Jessamine's proposed reappearance in Shropshire had been her suggestion, not his, but she was a determined young woman and Toni was sure it would not be long before she turned up on some pretext or other, especially now that Julian would come into his inheritance.

As soon as the funeral was over, Julian was closeted with the solicitors. He did not divulge what was being discussed. Edgar of course had willed everything to him with provision for Linda, but it was complicated by the number of taxes involved. Her aunt told Toni that it was doubtful if Julian could keep the estate intact.

'But he'll hang on to the house?' Toni asked anxiously. 'He couldn't part with Whiteladies?'

Linda sighed. 'It's much too big for just the two of us.'

But Julian would marry, he must marry now, if not Jessamine then some other girl. Toni viewed the local girls who came with their parents to call and offer condolences with a critical eye and decided they were an unprepossessing lot. Perhaps he would propose to Jessamine after all. She had much more style than the country girls had.

She was went up to London for her audition and was engaged for the part, being given a copy of the script to read before signing her contract. Lady Caroline's relentless pursuit of the poet evoked unpleasant echoes. Had she chased Julian with similar determination? But she had been too young to know what she was doing or

154

to realise that her feelings might not be returned. Nor did she have any other ties, so actually there was no parallel, only her sensitive pride had suggested it. The salary was generous, so she could not refuse it, and as she was not needed at once, she could return to White-ladies.

Linda and Julian expressed polite interest in her new venture. Her aunt said she had always understood Lady Caroline Lamb was fair, and Toni pointed out that if the director so decided she could either wear a wig or dye her hair.

'Don't you dare touch it!' Julian exclaimed with more energy than he had shown for many days. 'You'll spoil it. Your colouring is one of your assets.'

'So different from the Everards,' Toni remarked, eyeing him pensively.

They were seated at dinner, Julian for once being with them. From the wall behind her, Toni's great-great-grandfather, the first Sir Julian Everard, gazed down at her. Looking from the pictured face to her great-niece, Linda said:

'You're an Everard all right, in spite of the colouring. Family likenesses are most extraordinary. One never knows when they will suddenly become apparent. It's true Toni doesn't normally look like one, but when she came on in that play all dolled up at Mrs Higgins' tea-party, I did see a resemblance to old Sir Julian. It was something in the way she held her head and her nose and chin. Do you see what I mean, Julian?'

Julian glanced up at his forebear's rather grim countenance.

'I can't say I do.'

Linda rose from her place and moved behind Toni. She swept the hair off her forehead.

'Lift your chin, child. Now, look arrogant.'

Toni strove to comply.

Julian looked from her to the portrait.

'There is a certain similarity of feature,' he admitted.

'Edgar noticed it too,' Linda went on. 'He said the Everard stamp is very hard to eradicate, it turns up in generation after generation. It isn't noticeable in Toni because her colouring is so different, but it's there all right.'

'Thank you, Zia,' Toni said fervently.

'What for? The Everard genes?' Linda laughed as she resumed her seat. Then she sobered. 'He also said they're a dying race.'

Toni looked eagerly at Julian; he must accept Linda's remarks as proof of her parentage. His eyes were fixed upon her with a quizzical expression.

'So now you know, Toni,' he told her, 'though I shouldn't think you'd be flattered by being likened to him.' He indicated the portrait. 'Not that it's of any consequence, you're yourself, whoever your ancestors were, an individual in your own right.'

'But I'm glad to have proof that Lewis Everard was my father,' Toni cried.

Linda looked puzzled. 'Does anyone doubt it?'

'Yes.'

'How disgusting!' Linda proclaimed loudly.

Toni's eyes were still fixed upon Julian, but all he said was:

'People do have nasty minds, does it matter?'

Matter! When his doubts had caused her so much anguish.

She realised with a throb of indignation that what had been to her a devastating disclosure had held no real significance for him, or he would not have mentioned it to Jessamine. It had merely been a passing thought to account for her dissimilarity to the rest of her kin, and of no importance to him. It was her childish pride that had magnified it. But Jessamine had made his ill-considered words into a whip with which to chastise her: which he could never have dreamed she would do—not that, as he said, it mattered now, though Toni was glad to be reassured that she had a right to be sitting where she was an accredited member of the family.

'So you'll be going back to London?' Julian asked her. 'To achieve fresh triumphs.'

She searched his face for any sign of regret, but it was quite impassive. He did not care whether she went or stayed.

'They aren't going to start filming for a week or two,' she told them, 'so I can stay a bit longer.'

She glanced hopefully at Julian, but it was Linda who said:

'I'm so glad.'

Next morning Toni found Julian still at the breakfast table when she came down for her meal; usually he had gone out before she appeared. When she had finished her toast and marmalade, he asked her if she would come outside with him, as there was something he had to tell her.

She agreed at once, her mind full of conjectures and wild hopes. Was he going to say he had forgiven her and could she manage to eradicate the memory of their encounter at her flat? Hitherto he had avoided being alone with her, and their exchanges had been limited to the minimum of polite convention. Perhaps Linda's insistence that she was an Everard had made a difference after all.

He waited for her by the front door while she went to fetch a cardigan, for although it was a lovely day it was still only May and the breeze was chilly. He wore a tweed jacket and open shirt, looking very much the countryman. Toni looked slim and elegant in a white blouse and well cut pleated black skirt; her cardigan was black and white check.

He said almost apologetically: 'It's too nice a morning to stay in the house, don't you think? Shall we go and look at Dad's roses?'

The rose garden was full of memories for her—the night he had rejected her overtures, and the night she had overheard his conversation with Jessamine that had wrecked all her girlish dreams and changed her life. But all that seemed very far distant now. As they walked over the lawns from which the sun had not yet sucked all the dew, she glanced at his profile. He looked much older since his father's death, there were new lines from nose to mouth. She knew that he had been very much attached to Edgar and she longed to be able to comfort him and smooth the lines away with caressing hands. Hitherto she had never done anything to soothe or console him, only aggravate and try to tempt him along paths he did not wish to tread, so he would not look to her for solace now.

They passed through the iron gate and looked at the burgeoning buds. In another month the beds would be ablaze with colour.

'Dad created much beauty,' Julian said sadly, 'but I don't know what will become of it now.'

Startled, Toni stared at him. 'What do you mean? It's still here for you and your children.'

'If I ever have any, which I doubt. I am, as you reminded me the other day, middle-aged, or nearly so.'

Toni longed to be able to recall her ill-considered words. She had meant them to wound and they had, but she had been crazy when she uttered them. Hastily she sought to rescind them, exclaiming vehemently:

'Nonsense, Julian, you're still in your prime!'

'Not what you implied when I ...' He broke off. 'But that's not what I wanted to speak about, that's all finished and I hope we're both wiser.' Words that cut her to the heart. He looked away from her to the trees visible above the high wall sprouting with new green leaves. 'Whiteladies is to be sold,' he told her abruptly.

'Oh no!'

'I'm afraid so. It's too big to run economically. So long as the old man was alive we struggled to keep it going for his sake. Now there's no need.'

'But Zia, she'll hate to leave it.'

'She's reconciled. She's finding it a bit too much for her, now she's getting on. She's going to live with an old friend in Shrewsbury. What about your horse? You can't very well keep it in London, can you? Shall I dispose of it with the others?'

There was a finality about his words that dismayed her.

'But, Julian, what are you going to do?' she asked anxiously.

'Return to work. Farming isn't really my thing, Toni. I came back for my father's sake, but by the time all the duties and taxes are paid there won't be much left. I may keep a cottage for my retirement,' he smiled sadly, 'if I live to retirement age, but I shall try to get another assignment abroad, and if I go to Africa again, life's a bit uncertain there.'

Childishly she exclaimed: 'You said you'd go no more a-roaming.'

'That was when I had ... other plans,' he said curtly. 'Now there's nothing to keep me here.'

Other plans? Jessamine? But she was only too ready to accept him. Faintly Toni inquired:

'Your mother?'

'She understands. She'll absorb herself in good works.'

Toni sat down abruptly on a seat, overwhelmed by his news. Again her world was falling apart. Without Julian and Whiteladies her future looked bleak.

'You'll be all right, won't you?' Julian went on. 'You're doing so well in your profession. Mother will always take you in if anything goes wrong.'

She said nothing. Her eyes were fixed on a half opened rosebud. When it bloomed she would be far away. Julian of course could not leave at once, there would be a great deal to settle up first, but she would have no reason to come again. Her whole being rose in protest against what he proposed.

'Julian, you can't . . .'

'Can't what, dear?'

The endearment gave her courage. She could not, would not let him go out of her life.

'Leave me alone.' She raised dark imploring eyes to his face. 'Or if you must go, take me with you.'

She saw blank astonishment gather in his face, then the iron gate clanged. Startled, they looked towards it to see Jessamine Boycott coming into the rose garden. She ran towards Julian, her hands outstretched.

'I'm staying in Shrewsbury,' she explained breathlessly. 'So I thought I'd come. Oh, my poor dear, you're in trouble!' Her hands came to rest on his arm. 'Surely I can help?'

Toni rose to her feet. Jessamine had completely ignored her presence. Out of deference for their loss she was wearing a black well tailored trouser suit with touches of white at throat and wrists, which roused in Toni a feeling of outrage. Black and white were her own choice of colours, or rather lack of colour, and what right had Jessamine to mourn for Edgar? She did not, of course; she had come to lay claim to the new owner of Whiteladies, not knowing he intended to dispose of it.

Julian was speaking to her, thanking her for her solicitude. Toni walked out of the garden without looking back, regretting her impulsive outburst. She had asked Julian to take her with him, but Jessamine had intervened before he could reply. Perhaps the other girl had saved her from another rebuff, for she could hardly dare to hope he would have acceded to her request. Jessamine might be able to persuade him to stay in England, but that would be small consolation if he agreed to marry her.

Toni reach the house to find Jessamine's car parked before the front door and Linda in a flutter. The visitor must be invited to lunch.

'She found Julian?' she asked.

'Yes, I left them together.'

'Oh, did you?' Her aunt looked doubtfully at Toni's set face. 'I thought that was all off, but apparently it's on again.'

'So it seems.' Toni was non-committal.

'Well, if they do become engaged, I hope she'll manage to keep him in England. You know he's talking of going abroad again, and I'd so much rather he didn't. They could live in London. I never thought Jessamine was really a country girl, and of course Julian won't be penniless apart from what he earns. They could be very comfortable.'

Every word was like a blow upon Toni's heart. Linda had always approved of Jessamine and saw in her reappearance the rebirth of her hopes.

'Oh, no doubt,' she agreed. 'I shan't be in for lunch, Zia. I'm going for a ride.'

'But, my dear, Miss Boycott will be here ...'

161

'She won't miss me,' Toni declared bitterly. 'She'd rather have my room than my company. I and the nice Miss Boycott don't see eye to eye.'

She ran upstairs to change into her riding gear, and Linda watched her go with troubled eyes. She was not as unperceptive as her niece supposed.

Toni sat on the craggy outcrop on the top of the Long Mynd, where she had first declared her love for Julian. She had taken off her mount's saddle and bridle and allowed the horse to graze, knowing it would come to her when she whistled to it. They had travelled a long way and it was a long distance back, so the beast must have a rest before they returned.

The hills were clothed in a mantle of fresh green, the bracken fronds uncurling, the heather pushing up new shoots. Mentally she was reviewing her short tempestuous life from the moment she first met her great-aunt in the Whiteladies sitting room to the present hour. Julian—always Julian, but now she would have to put him out of her life for ever. Either he would marry the 'nice girl' she so detested, or he would go off to some foreign country, possibly for years. Either way she would lose him irrevocably. In spite of their estrangement she had hoped that something would happen to bring them together again. In her heart of hearts she could not really believe that the bond between them could be broken. Now she knew that had only been wishful thinking.

The only time that Julian had sought her out since she had come to Shropshire was to tell her he was selling their home. He was deeply grieved by the loss of his father, and if only she had not been so obsessed by her insane desire for revenge against a slight which as he had said the other night was of no importance she might have been the one to comfort him.

Now Jessamine had come to hand out sympathy and would catch him in his vulnerable hour. When he had brought Toni to this very spot where she was sitting, she had been a child too young to grapple with emotions too strong for her. If only she had known then all that Ambrose had taught her, but how could she, an over-emotional sixteen-year-old? Now she was a woman it was too late. She would survive and make some sort of life for herself and in time Julian's image would fade, but he would take a part of her with him whoever he married and wherever he went, and she would never be wholly whole again.

As the shadows lengthened over the hills, she judged Jessamine would have departed. She had eaten nothing since breakfast, but felt no desire for food, not realising that her terrible sense of emptiness was partly physical hunger. As she resaddled her horse, she caressed its glossy neck. When Julian had first suggested parting with it she had resolved that somehow she would contrive to keep it, but that would not be easy. It would be wiser to let it go, as everything else would go with the loss of Whiteladies. She swung herself into the saddle wondering if she would be met with the news of Julian's engagement when she reached home. If she were she would go back to London on the morrow. It was nearly dusk when she stabled her horse, in the long spring twilight. She met her aunt in the hall, and Linda looked relieved at the sight of her, exclaiming:

'Where have you been? I thought something must have happened to you.'

'I've been up the Long Mynd,' Toni told her.

'Heavens, that's a long way! You might have told me where you were going if you were going to be out so late. If Julian had been here I'd have sent him to look

163

for you. Someone would have seen you, I suppose, but he's gone into Shrewsbury.'

Toni blenched. 'With Miss Boycott?' she asked faintly.

'No, oh no. She left after lunch.' Linda was diverted from the subject of Toni's truancy. 'They talked for a long time alone together. She seemed a little distraite over lunch, a good sign, don't you think? But she said she couldn't stay when I offered to put her up for the night. If only Julian would make up his mind!'

'Hasn't he?' asked Toni.

'I don't know.'

'Then perhaps you could ask him.'

'I can't. Julian's always so cagey about his girl-friends. If you get a chance do try to persuade him that that's where his happiness lies. A wife and family would give him an object in life and cure his wanderlust.'

Toni smiled. She did not believe Julian would be happy with Jessamine.

'If you can't persuade him I'm sure he wouldn't listen to me,' she declared.

'I'm not so sure.' Linda looked at her great-niece thoughtfully. 'He thinks a lot of you, you know. He used to keep a photograph of you in his wallet. I saw it once when he was looking for his credit card.'

Used to keep! He would have burned it by now.

'He regards me as a sort of protégée after pulling me out of the ruins in Italy,' Toni said lightly. 'But I can't intervene in his love life, he might suspect my motives.'

Linda's glance was shrewd. 'You had a bit of a crush on him yourself, as the schoolgirls say, when you were a teenager. I've sometimes thought he was waiting for you to grow up.'

Toni turned away. 'What a funny idea, Zia, Julian and me!' She laughed forcedly. 'An incongruous couple! I suppose you've had dinner. I'll go and forage for something in the kitchen.'

So Linda was not as blind as she had thought, and Julian had carried her photograph about with him. If only she had handled their affair with more sophistication she might have won her heart's desire.

'I had about as much finesse as a bulldozer,' she thought despondently as she helped herself to bread and cheese. 'And now I've killed any affection he had for me.'

She went upstairs and bathed, but felt too restless to sleep. A May moon was flooding the garden with silver light as it had done on that fateful night that now seemed so long ago. Putting on slacks and a thin sweater, Toni went out into its radiance. Linda had gone to her room and a light showed behind her bedroom curtains, so she was not yet asleep. Julian must have told her that he meant to give up Whiteladies, but she had not spoken of it. Perhaps now she had lost her husband she would be glad to leave it and its memories to start a new life amid the amenities of a town. As her son had said, even if he had stayed the house was too big for just the two of them.

Though it was nearly midnight, he had not come home. Toni went to look if his car was in the garage, but it was not. She suspected that in spite of what Linda had said, he had met Jessamine in Shrewsbury and that was why he was so late. He did not want to pursue his courtship under his mother's inquisitive eyes. The thought depressed her. She strolled away from the garage towards the back of the house where the bricked-up arch had given rise to the sinister legend. Idly she glanced towards it, and then she froze. Some neighbouring bushes threw wavering shadows over the wall, stirred by the night breeze, and in the mingling of white light and shade a wraithlike form took shape against the archway. Toni did not believe in ghosts, and reason told her it must be some trick of the light, but all the same her scalp prickled and a cold shiver ran down her spine. The figure did look like a white nun, its head bowed, obscured by its hooded cowl. Toni stood rooted to the spot unable to move waiting for the wraith to dissolve.

'*Amor vincit omnia.*'

She did not know if the words were actually spoken, but they were conveyed to her brain. Love conquers all, a mediaeval nun would naturally know Latin, and it was nice to know the White Lady could still believe that after her gruesome death. Was she trying to suggest that Toni's long love for Julian would win in the end? Absurd, of course, there was not anything there; either she was dreaming or the victim of an hallucination.

Even while these thoughts flitted through Toni's mind, the figure slowly began to raise its head. Sheer atavistic terror of the supernatural submerged Toni's common sense. She dreaded to see what the moonlight might reveal beneath the hood, a human face or the skull of one long departed.

Afterwards she was to wish she had stood her ground and discovered if she were being hoaxed or whether the visitant really was a ghost, but that she would never know, for a surge of panic swept through her and with an inarticulate cry she ran, straight into the path of an oncoming car.

The driver uttered a startled oath as he slammed on his brakes. Julian was going very slowly, nosing towards the garage, and it was as much the impetus of Toni's flight as the speed of the car that sent her rolling as the wing struck her. She lay a crumpled heap in a patch of moonlight. Dimly she was aware of someone

166

stooping over her, of an anguished voice crying: 'Toni ... Toni darling! My God, I've killed her!' Then all was blank.

Toni recovered consciousness to find that she was lying in her own bed and the local doctor, a gruff but kindly personality, was bending over her, saying:

'No bones broken, luckily, possibly a slight concussion, but I don't think there's any serious injury.'

Toni opened her eyes and grinned up at him. He went on:

'Well, miss, so you've come back to us. Where do you feel it?'

Toni moved and winced. 'Here.' She indicated the place.

'Yes, you'll have a beautiful bruise when it comes out,' the small eyes twinkled in the weatherbeaten face, 'but you'll do. You can thank your lucky stars it's no worse.'

'But what hit me?'

'Everard's car. He thought he'd killed you.'

Toni saw then that Julian was standing behind the doctor, looking distraught, his usually tidy hair standing on end as if he had run his fingers through it repeatedly.

'I didn't see him, didn't even know he was there,' she explained.

'So it seems,' Julian said curtly. 'What on earth were you doing rushing about outside at midnight and not looking where you were going?'

'You shouldn't have been coming home so late,' she retorted, noticing he was wearing his best suit. She must be right—Jessamine had delayed her departure so that he could meet her in Shrewsbury, in spite of what Linda had said. He was unlikely to have had a business appointment so late. 'You didn't sound your horn,' she concluded.

'I didn't expect anyone to come running full tilt round the corner as if all the devils in hell were after them,' he snapped. He was restraining strong emotion and the effort made him abrupt, but Toni only noticed his annoyance.

'Not a devil but a ghost,' she announced. 'I saw the White Lady.'

Julian looked at the doctor in consternation.

'Good God, she's wandering!'

'Oh no, I'm not. I saw her quite plainly.' Toni's eyes were liquid jet in her white face as she stared challengingly at Julian. 'She had a message for me.'

'Don't talk any more, dear.' It was Linda's soothing voice, and Toni realised that she also was present. She was wearing her dressing gown and must have been roused when Julian brought her in. 'You're over-excited.'

'But I did see her,' Toni insisted, moving her head impatiently on her pillows. 'After all she's supposed to haunt this place, isn't she? And someone,' (she knew it had been Jessamine but did not want to mention her name) '... said I was the one most likely to see her. Don't you want to hear what she said, Julian?'

'The girl's got too vivid an imagination,' the doctor intervened. 'Silly superstitious nonsense,' he went on with a growl. 'She'd better have a sedative. I'll give you something for her to take, Mrs Everard.' He reached for his bag.

Toni ignored him, her eyes were still fixed on Julian. 'Don't you, Julian?'

'What was it?' he asked, humouring her.

'*Amor vincit omnia.*'

His eyes flickered. 'Applicable to whom, do you sup-

168

pose?' he inquired blandly.

Disappointed, Toni closed her eyes. She had hoped for a more definite reaction, after the emotion she had heard in his voice when he picked her up, but perhaps she had imagined that too. All he was expressing now was barely concealed impatience with her folly.

The doctor handed Linda a box of pills.

'Give her two of these,' he said. 'They'll make her sleep. I'll look in in the morning, but I don't anticipate any ill effects beyond the bruising.' He turned to Toni. 'Now, miss, forget about your ghost and her cryptic messages and have a nice restful sleep. Can't have you getting neurotic, you know! Goodnight.'

He gave her a singularly sweet smile that belied his gruff tone.

Julian went with him to see him out and Linda departed to fetch a glass of water. Left alone, Toni sought to reconstruct what had happened. She recalled her frozen terror when the apparition had lifted its head and her panic flight, and regretted it. She should have stayed and ascertained if the thing was tangible. She had not even seen Julian's car when it knocked her down. All she could recall was his frantic voice calling her name. Had it really been Julian speaking, or was the second voice also a delusion as she thought the nun's must have been? He had sounded as if he cared ... and cared deeply, but when she had come round his tone had been admonitory, pointing out that the accident had been her own fault, and her pathetic attempt to win a response from him by repeating the nun's words had been neatly riposted. Toni sighed; it seemed to be impossible to reach him.

Linda returned with a glass of water and offered it to her with the pills.

'Where's Julian?' Toni demanded.

'Having a drink,' Linda replied. 'He needed it. You gave him a nasty shock, you know, running into him like that so heedlessly.'

'I suppose I did,' Toni agreed. A gleam of malice showed in her eyes. 'But a stiff whisky will soon put him right. He might have been more sympathetic—after all, I'm the one who got hurt.'

'My dear, he was most upset. You looked ghastly when he brought you in and he was terrified that you were badly injured. He wouldn't leave you while we waited for the doctor, and kept saying over and over again—'If she's crippled I'll never forgive myself, never,' although I assured him I didn't think there was any serious damage. You mustn't grudge him a reviver.'

'I don't.' Toni was heartened by this revelation. At first Julian's recourse to the whisky bottle had seemed callous, but if he had really been so anxious it was understandable.

Linda gave her great-niece a long penetrating look.

'Julian's devoted to you,' she told her. 'I believe that's why he can't make up his mind to marry Jessamine.'

'Oh, Zia!' Toni's face shone with sudden radiance. 'But he said he's going away,' she added despondently.

'He thinks you're absorbed in your career,' Linda said, 'and of course you're too young for him.'

'I'm not!' Toni wailed. 'He's always made such a mountain out of that age gap. As if it mattered!' She sat up abruptly. 'Ask him to come and say goodnight before I take those pills,' she commanded imperiously.

She was elated by her aunt's words and felt sure that if she could see Julian now, while he was upset by the accident, she might be able to wring from him a promise not to leave her, or at least persuade him to take her with him if he went abroad.

Linda shook her head. 'You must wait until the morning,' she said firmly. 'You must calm down now.' For Toni's black eyes were glowing. 'Besides,' she went on disapprovingly, 'your bedroom isn't the right place for emotional scenes.'

'Oh, rats,' Toni exclaimed, 'don't be so conventional! He's seen me in bed before often enough.'

'When you were a child,' Linda reminded her. 'You're grown up now.'

'Thank goodness you've realised it!' Toni lay back on her pillows and regarded her aunt thoughtfully. 'You dislike emotional scenes wherever they are, don't you? You think they're bad form.'

'One should always be dignified,' Linda declared. 'The right place for scenes is on the stage.'

'But Shakespeare said "All the world's a stage",' Toni countered rebelliously.

'So he did, but you must keep quiet,' Linda admonished her. 'No scenes of any sort tonight or you'll be running a temperature. Now take your dope and go to sleep. Julian won't run away.'

But that was just what he was contemplating doing, but he could not go yet. Toni swallowed the pills and was already asleep when Julian came softly to her door to see how she was.

Together mother and son contemplated her pale face surrounded by the black mass of her hair. Her long eyelashes made fans on her wan cheeks. In sleep she looked like a child again.

'If only she were older,' Julian sighed.

'She never was all that young,' Linda murmured. 'Her experience in Italy ripened her too soon; we didn't understand.'

Toni stirred in her sleep. 'Julian,' she whispered, and sank into deeper slumber. The two watchers exchanged glances and quietly stole out of the room.

CHAPTER TEN

Toni awoke next morning with a sense of glad expectancy. Linda's words of the night before had sent her spirits soaring. Surely now she could break down the barriers of Julian's obstinacy—if his mother were right, and she did not think she could be mistaken. Self-contained as the Everards were, they did not lack insight, and Linda must know her son better than anyone else did.

To her great disgust her aunt insisted that she must stay in bed until the doctor had called, but when she went to the bathroom she had to admit she was more shaky than she had supposed. Julian, she was told, was out on the farm, having been informed that she was still sleeping. He had not waited to hear the doctor's verdict or discover for himself that she was all right. That was ominous and Toni's exhilaration began to evaporate, though it was possible he shared Linda's sense of propriety. Since he was assured that she was not badly injured, he had decided it was not correct to visit her when she was in bed. Julian had these odd reticences, which were so out of keeping with modern casual behaviour, but Toni felt he was overdoing it. She had a lurking fear that his conduct stemmed from indifference.

She thought wistfully of the slit of a dressing room that she had first occupied that had had access to his, and she sighed for the intimacy of her childhood days, which seemed unlikely ever to recur, for when Linda had declared that her son was devoted to Toni, she had not known what had happened in London and that Julian had much to forgive. Nor did either of them know what had transpired between him and Jessamine on the previous day, and more especially during the evening if he had been coming back from seeing her in Shrewsbury, for his late return was still unexplained.

Despondently Toni picked up the script of the Byron film which was on the table beside her bed. She was under contract to do that series and could not get out of it, but she felt no enthusiasm about it. It was a means of paying her bills, that was all. The infatuated Lady Caroline Lamb had described Lord Byron as mad, bad and dangerous to know. If only Julian had been madder, badder and dangerous! Then she would not be lying desolate upon her virginal bed. He had never denied the strong physical attraction between them, only resisted it. Such scruples were outmoded in this permissive age, she decided, but she would not have him different. He would not be Julian if he were less honourable, only it was frustrating.

The doctor came and examined her again—unnecessarily, Toni thought, but he overruled her objections by reminding her that she was too valuable a person to run any risks.

'Our most promising juvenile actress,' he said smugly, and prescribed a day in bed. 'To get over the shock.'

As soon as he had gone, Toni got up and dressed. It was another lovely day and she was not going to waste it indoors. Linda remonstrated with her, but though, had she been honest, she would have had to admit that her bruised side was painful, she persisted in going outside.

She wore slacks and a knitted top in her favourite green, which blended with the fresh emerald of the grass and trees. Shrubs and bushes were heavy with blossom, lilacs, laburnums and cherry in the grounds, and the white froth of hawthorn bloom in the hedgerows. The most beautiful time of year, Toni thought, wondering where Julian had gone. She found him eventually on the headland of a cornfield, which was edged by the copse into which she had run for refuge on the night when he had told Jessamine of his doubt about her parentage. It had been sown with winter wheat and the new growth was a foot high, a weaving mass of verdant green blades. Julian was surveying it with satisfaction, for it was a fine healthy crop.

He was unaware of her presence for she came up behind him, until she spoke his name, and he swung round to face her.

'Toni! But should you be up and about?'

'Oh, I'm fine,' she said impatiently. 'The doctor's an old fusspot, and Zia's another. Who could stay indoors on a day like this?'

'Not you, obviously.' His eyes went from her over the cultivated fields to the distant horizon, a faint blue line of hills. 'England is perfect this weather. It wasn't until I'd spent years in the desert that I realised what a beautiful, restful colour green is.'

'Yet you want to go back?'

He smiled. 'It also has its charm.'

'Can you really tear yourself away from Whiteladies?' she asked earnestly. 'The farm is doing so well. Must you give it up?'

He shrugged his shoulders.

'Needs must when the devil drives. I'm not really keen on agriculture, though I don't think I've done so badly during my stewardship.' He looked complacently at the growing corn.

Toni was not interested in the wheat; Julian was being tiresomely impersonal.

'Where were you last night?' she asked abruptly, for

the question was pertinent. 'You don't usually come home so late.'

'I was entertaining a prospective purchaser,' he told her. 'Why so inquisitive, little one?'

'I wondered if you were with Jessamine,' she said bluntly.

'Oh, she went off in the afternoon. After I'd told her I had to sell Whiteladies, she lost interest.' He spoke drily.

Emboldened by that welcome news, Toni inquired: 'Would you really have cared if I'd been killed last night? I mean really cared.'

The question was melodramatic, possibly foolish, and she watched his face eagerly for his reaction. It was all she had hoped.

'Good God, Toni, what a thing to say!' He exploded. 'Of course I'd have cared. It's too dreadful to contemplate!'

'Even though I'm so aggravating?' she asked archly.

'Don't be childish,' he said roughly.

'Yes, you've always thought of me as a child,' she observed. 'A precocious, tiresome child who tried to overthrow your conventional standards.' She glanced timidly at his set face. 'You aren't really middle-aged, Julian.'

'Approaching forty,' he said sombrely.

'That's the prime of life!'

He suddenly gripped her shoulders and his eyes were flickering blue flame.

'What do you want now, little witch?' he demanded hoarsely. 'Haven't you caused enough havoc in my life?'

'Have I caused havoc?' Her eyes were limpid dark pools.

'Of course you have—Delilah, Circe, Lilith, Messalina, all the sirens of history and mythology rolled into one. God knows how I've managed to resist you.'

'But why must you resist me?' Toni asked softly. 'Or call me all those horrid names? Oh, Julian, Julian, I've always loved you so since that first moment when you came into our cottage in Italy, like ... like a young god. I've tried so hard to make myself worthy of you, that wretched school ... trying to be a ... a lady. But it wasn't any good, you preferred Jessamine.'

All her acquired sophistication fell away from her, she was a child again, a pleading passionate child. Julian's hands dropped from her shoulders and he turned away from her.

'I've always loved you, Toni,' he said gently. 'First as a child and later, as a woman, but it was so unsuitable. If I'd taken you, married you, a child bride!' He laughed ruefully. 'It would have been unfair to you. When your ... your infatuation died, you would have found yourself chained to an ageing man. God knows I wanted you, but when you reminded me of the gap between us in your flat I thought you'd learned at last to love a younger man.'

'I don't want a younger man, I only want you, there'll never be anyone but you. No one else has ever touched my heart, man or woman. Even Zia has always been remote. Oh, don't you understand, you blind bat?' Her rich voice deepened with passionate urgency. 'There's no happiness for me apart from you, and if you go away again, Africa or whatever, I shall wish you had killed me last night.'

'Toni!' Very gently he drew her into his arms as if she were something infinitely precious. A glint of humour showed in his eyes. 'But what about what you said to me in the flat—you weren't loving me then, were you?'

'Yes,' she said, 'but I'd been so hurt. I overheard you

tell Jessamine that you didn't think Lewis Everard was my father ... I thought that was why you despised me ... an Italian by-blow.'

She felt him wince. 'Despise you? Never!' he exclaimed. 'It didn't matter who your father was, you are you, yourself, as I said the other night, a bewitching, beautiful, talented girl.'

'Why did you doubt that Daddy was my father?'

'Not only the difference in looks, but you were so vivid and ardent to be old Lewis's daughter. He was such a nondescript person, but Mother put that right when she saw your resemblance to Sir Julian. Grim old party he was too—were you flattered, darling?'

'Relieved,' she told him. 'It mayn't have mattered to you, but to me it seemed awful, as if I didn't belong anywhere.'

'My poor sweet!'

He said then how sorry he was for his indiscretion, but of course he had no idea that she was listening, and he had thought Jessamine was a safe confidant.

'No woman is safe where getting her man is concerned,' Toni observed drily. 'Jessamine disapproved of me and feared you might be attracted to me.'

'How right she was!'

'Exactly, she threw it up at me afterwards.'

'The bitch!' he exclaimed.

'But you liked her,' she reminded him. 'You contemplated marrying her.'

'But I couldn't. That was why I went off to Africa instead of joining her in Scotland. I couldn't go through with it when I was obsessed by you. That night in the rose garden you were never nearer to being seduced, my darling, except perhaps in the flat.' He laughed. 'I told you then you needed looking after, but you scorned me.'

'What a pair of idiots we've been,' she murmured. 'But I don't want to be looked after, Julian, I want to be loved. You'll stay with me? You won't run away again?'

His hold tightened. 'I couldn't now even if I wanted too. Oh, Toni, Toni darling!' He buried his face in her hair.

They came back to a smiling Linda who was expecting their news.

'I don't really approve of cousins marrying,' she said, 'but Toni is once removed, which makes a difference.' She looked at the girl's radiant face. Happiness made Toni breathtakingly beautiful. 'You've been very faithful and persistent, my child. You deserved to get him in the end.'

'In fact she was a brazen little hussy,' Julian said, laughing, but his eyes were very tender. 'I can hardly believe my luck, and that this isn't one of the fantasies I used to create away in the desert.'

'All your own fault,' Toni told him severely. 'You'd only to tell me you were waiting for me to grow up and we'd both have been happy.'

'I was convinced you'd change your mind when you were older.'

Toni gave him a reproachful look and Linda intervened.

'What about your profession?' she asked doubtfully. 'You won't want to give that up?'

Toni shrugged her shoulders. 'It doesn't mean a lot to me. I'll have to do the Byron serial, of course, but after that I mean to devote myself to being a good wife ... and mother.'

All the Italian in her gave priority to husband and family. The glance she gave Julian caused his eyes to gleam.

Her decision pleased Julian; he had no wish to be separated from her while she fulfilled professional engagements. He had to complete the sale of Whiteladies and find work in England, and with his qualifications there would not be much difficulty about that. They decided that provisionally their wedding would take place next spring.

'It's a long time to wait,' Julian said regretfully, 'but it would be wise to wait until I've fixed up my affairs and you've completed your contract. Then we can go straight into a settled home.'

Toni agreed it would be sensible, but half-heartedly. So much could happen in a year's time. She uneasily suspected that in spite of his assurances he was regretting parting with Whiteladies. It had sheltered his family for so many generations, but there seemed no way in which he could keep it. He had declared that the old must give way to the new, and the days of the county squires was over. He had no wish to be an anachronism, but Toni was sure he grieved.

The day before Toni was due to return to London, Mr Boycott came to call. Toni had never met him before. He was a masculine version of his daughter, with the same grey-blue eyes and fresh complexion, growing a little stout, as Jessamine would probably do unless she dieted carefully. He was a very successful property dealer and was interested in the estate. Julian had practically disposed of it, but the contract was not yet signed and Mr Boycott made him a better offer.

He stayed to lunch, but left immediately afterwards. Linda was all agog to know the reason for his coming. Julian joined her and Toni in the sitting room after he had seen the visitor off. He looked round the gracious room with a wistful expression and Toni was aware of a sinking heart; she had a premonition that

Mr Boycott's offer was somehow connected with his daughter, and though she was reconciled to leaving the place, she resented the thought of Jessamine living there, that was if her father intended to purchase it.

'So he wants to buy Whiteladies?' Linda inquired. 'That's why he came, isn't it? Did he offer a lot more than the other fellow?'

'He did, but there were strings attached.'

Toni looked at Julian questioningly, but he evaded meeting her eyes.

'He imagines Jess and I are engaged,' Julian went on in a curiously flat voice. 'She must have misled him. I didn't get a chance to deny it, he was so full of his plans. His idea is that she and I should live here and of course our children would inherit the property. He pointed out that it had always belonged to the Everards and Everards should continue to live here. The man seems to be rolling even in these days. He would allow us, or rather her, sufficient income to run it properly. Jess wouldn't mind if you, Mother, continued to live with us.'

Dead silence followed his words. Linda's gaze was fixed on a bunch of lilac in a china vase. Toni knew intuitively what she was thinking—if only Julian had adhered to his original intentions she would not have to leave her home. Toni looked anywhere but at Julian. He was being bribed to marry Jessamine, and the bait dangled before him must be tempting. That young woman had always been set upon acquiring Whiteladies, but she wanted Julian with it. He had the choice between retaining his ancestral home and her dowerless self. He had not apparently contradicted Mr Boycott's belief that he was engaged to his daughter, and surely he would have found an opportunity to do so unless he was considering his offer.

Presently she rose to her feet.

'I expect you'd like to discuss it with Zia,' she said, and was amazed that she managed to speak so calmly.

'There's nothing to discuss,' Julian returned shortly.

'I think there is. I know, in spite of all you've said, how you both love this house.' Toni made her way blindly to the door. 'You're still free, Julian, our engagement has not been announced.'

She went swiftly straight out of the front door, running over the lawns to the rose garden. Love—what was love? Everybody declared it did not last, but property did. Whiteladies had stood for several hundred years. Everards had lived there for most of them. It was not as if Julian were repelled by Jessamine. He liked her, and he had thought of marrying her once; he would not find it difficult to be reconciled to her, if there were no obstacle.

Toni paced distractedly up and down the paved paths noting mechanically that the roses, Edgar's roses, were already coming into bloom, yellow, red, pink and white; floribundas, standards and the climbers up the wall. So much beauty that could be Julian's for the rest of his life if she were not in the way. At this moment Linda would be pointing out all the advantages of the match. He had told her that she had played havoc with his life, and now he had the chance to re-organise it in the way it should go. In spite of the Socialistic trend, this was where the Everards belonged, the leading family in the neighbourhood. I shouldn't have intervened, she thought sadly. I tried to take him from Jessamine and I succeeded, but true love puts the beloved's happiness first. He'll never be happy with me now knowing what he's had to relinquish for my sake. I've always been an alien here, the poppy among the corn. The White Lady was wrong, love does not conquer all things, money does.

She left the rose garden intent upon returning to London at once. She could pack her bag and hire a car in the village to take her to the station. The local garage ran a taxi service. Somehow she must get away without seeing Julian. He would oppose her decision, she was sure, but he would come to be grateful to her. She would write to him from London and tell him she had reconsidered and decided that she did not want to give up her profession after all, and that Linda was right, they were too near kin to marry.

She heard Julian calling her and hid in the bushes while he went past. He would look for her in the fields, perhaps believing she had again sought refuge in the little wood. It would take quite a while for him to search it, and give her time to regain the house. In frantic haste she threw a few things into a suitcase, checked the money in her handbag and crept out of the back door. No one saw her go.

Toni reached London that evening having caught a fast train. The flat was empty, for Ellen had been given a holiday, on the understanding that Toni would contact her when she decided to come back. The telephone rang as she entered it, but fearing it might be Julian she did not answer it. As it continued to ring at intervals, she took the receiver off the hook. He would think she was not there. Later she rang Annabel, suggesting that if she were not engaged they might meet. She could not bear her solitude and her painful thoughts. Annabel was surprised.

'I thought you were still in the country.'

'I had to come back and I'm lonely,' Toni confessed. 'Be a good pal and take pity on me.'

Annabel told her that she was going to a night club,

but if she liked Toni could join her and her escort, whom she would ring and ask to bring another man.

'If it's not too frivolous ... I mean ... er ...'

'You think I'm in mourning?' Toni returned. 'That's just it, I'm so miserable I need cheering up. I'm not conventional, you know, and my aunt won't know.'

But it was not Edgar's death that was making her miserable, nor did she appear so when she joined Annabel and the two young men—Annabel's friend had found an unattached male. She wore a long black dress, that left her beautiful neck and arms bare, with a white stole, and her gaiety was hectic. The young man Annabel had managed to find for her was dazzled, congratulating himself that he had been free when his friend rang up, thus finding himself partnering the glamorous Antonia Alderley, who was usually so un-approachable. He had been told his blind date was a charming girl, but he had not expected anyone so spectacular.

The night club was nothing very special, a little place with the usual dim lighting, a small space for dancing, tables and a bar, and somewhat indifferent cabaret. Annabel, who seldom went to such places, declared it was super, but Toni hardly noticed her surroundings. She danced once or twice with her escort, unaware of his close clasp. Mind and heart were far away.

Over a glass of champagne which he insisted upon buying for her, he asked her about her new role. Toni laughed.

'Another sexy bitch. Type-casting, you know.'

The young man looked slightly shocked.

'But you're not ...'

'Aren't I?' She gave him a provocative look. 'You don't know me.'

'May I hope that one day I shall?'

'You may hope,' she returned indifferently. He was a smooth slick type and she had no intention of seeing him again.

He took her home in the early hours, and she had some difficulty in repelling his amorous advances in the taxi.

'I didn't expect you'd be cold,' he complained.

'Oh, I am, my heart's made of ice,' she told him. 'Be content, Harry. (That was his name, his surname she never grasped.) You've had the honour of entertaining a famous actress, but I never smooch in taxis.'

'I thought you said you were a sexy bitch.'

'I said I was cast for one. I seem to give that impression, but appearances are so misleading.'

They reached the block of flats, and Toni told him:

'Forgive me for not asking you in, but I'm very tired.'

She had had quite enough of Harry.

'At least let me see you to your door,' he insisted.

'That's not necessary, thank you, and there's no lift,' she told him, hoping to discourage him. 'There are quite a lot of stairs.'

'Then my escort is necessary. Quite a lot of things can happen ... on stairs. At least let me stay with you until you've opened your door and made sure all is as it should be.'

Toni sighed and led the way up to the first floor, unimpressed by this ingenious gallantry. Somehow she must prevent him from actually entering her flat and discovering that she was alone in it. As they walked down the corridor towards it, a tall figure detached itself from the shadows beyond her door and stood barring their way.

'Julian!' Toni exclaimed in dismayed surprise.

She had thought he had been trying to contact her on the telephone, but she had never expected that he

184

would follow her to London. He looked as if he might have been waiting for some time, for having no key he could not get in. But what must he be thinking of her for having obviously been out enjoying herself so shortly after their joint bereavement, and in male company too? Impossible to make him understand the desperate loneliness that had driven her to seek such diversion without betraying her need of him, which would be unwise, in his own interests, and a wound to her pride. Now he had seen what she had been doing, he would probably leave in disgust without waiting for any explanation, and it would be better so.

Harry was looking daggers at this good-looking man whom Toni had greeted by his first name, while Julian's eyes turned to blue ice as they rested upon him. Toni determined to make the best of the situation, though she did not like to think he would believe her to be heartless.

'I didn't expect you,' she said with her best social manner, as she fumbled in her handbag for her key. 'I hope you haven't been waiting long.'

'Long enough,' he returned curtly. '*I* didn't *expect* to find you out.'

Inwardly she quailed at his condemnatory tone, but she said vaguely:

'Yes ... well, there was a reason for that.' She put her key in the lock, and as the door swung open, turned to Harry with a sweet smile. 'Come in for a drink, won't you?' she invited.

'I think not.' Julian's voice was as icy as his eyes. 'Your friend will I'm sure excuse you. You look tired out, and I'm sure he won't want to intrude upon family business.'

Without giving Harry a chance to speak, he pushed

Toni unceremoniously into the flat and closed the door in the young man's face.

Toni had meant to use Harry's presence as a screen between herself and Julian's anger. Defeated in that purpose, she nevertheless expostulated as she switched on the light in her sitting room.

'That was very high-handed of you, Julian.'

She drew the curtains over the windows with a calmness she was far from feeling, for Julian was standing in the middle of the room watching her with a grim expression under lowering brows. As he did not speak, she added: 'How did you know I was back here?'

'There was nowhere else you were likely to go except the Thornes'. I rang up Mrs Thorne as soon as I found this place deserted and she said you'd come back and gone out on the town with her daughter. That did surprise me, under the circumstances.'

'I couldn't stand sitting here moping alone,' she flashed, roused to temper by his acid tone. 'Ellen isn't back yet.'

'Is she not?' His tone became smooth as silk. 'What an opportunity! So you brought that young whelp back to entertain you.'

'I had no such intention! Annabel made up a foursome and he was only seeing me home. I was thankful to be rid of him.'

'You sounded it when you asked him in.'

She turned away with a weary gesture.

'Julian, do you mind? I . . . can't stand any more.' She felt quite incapable of coping with his censure. 'I'm very tired.'

His face softened as he surveyed her drooping figure. She looked very young and slightly pathetic, her head bowed under the weight of her hair, her hands crossed on her breast holding the white stole over her naked shoulders. Like a young Madonna in a painting by an old master, he thought, but his tone was harsh when he spoke.

'Not surprising, rushing up to town and coming back in the small hours.' He moved towards her purposefully, and Toni turned round to face him, head raised defiantly.

'What I do is my affair, not yours.'

'That I question. I suppose this is the sequel to your announcement that I was free. As if I could ever be free from you, Toni.' A throb of passion entered his voice. 'You little fool, how could you imagine I'd take Boycott's proposition seriously?'

'Why not? It seemed very sensible to me. A way to secure Whiteladies in perpetuity.'

'As if I'd want it on those terms! Let me tell you this, whoever I sell the place to, it won't be Boycott, even if he offers the earth. I want nothing more to do with that family. Jess is a double-dealer.'

Toni stifled a surge of triumph. He might be peeved with Jessamine at the moment, but he would forgive her when he considered that her misrepresentations had been made for love of him.

'Come here,' Julian commanded imperiously, as she said nothing.

Toni edged further away from him, shaking her head. She could not believe that Julian was so ready to part with his birthright, he had not yet fully considered the matter and seeing her with Harry had awoken his possessive jealousy. Somehow she must persuade him that he would not be happy married to herself at the price of losing his home. Later he would recall that he might have kept it if it had not been for her. Thus for the first time in their joint history she sought to relinquish all claim to his affection, putting what she believed was

187

his best interests before her own.

'Julian, I'm sorry,' she said earnestly, moving towards him. 'I've been so very wrong to cling to you. I've decided our marriage would be a great mistake for many reasons. I . . .'

She got no further. He seized her in a close constricting embrace, and his mouth closed her lips. Whatever resolutions she had made, Toni was not proof against physical contact. Her arms went round his neck, and she clung to him with all the passionate response of her being. He kissed her throat, her bare shoulders, his lips lingering over the smooth satin of her skin, and finally her mouth again, so hard and demanding that it was bruised. Finally he picked her up and dropped her on the couch. Standing over her, he decreed:

'The programme is changed. There will be no waiting for our wedding. I'll get a special licence, and I can quite well live here with you until everything is settled. You're going to have no further opportunities of running round town with slick specimens like the one you picked up this evening. Besides, after tonight, and there's not much of tonight left, you'll be hopelessly compromised. No, not a word,' as she started to protest. 'I don't know what maggot you got into your silly little brain that caused you to bolt, but you'll never run away again. Whether you like it or not, I'm staying here from now on to make sure you behave yourself.'

Toni was delighted by this assumption of masculine arrogance. She capitulated with heart felt relief.

'Whatever you say, O Lord and Master,' she agreed submissively.

'Maintain that attitude and ours'll be a happy marriage,' Julian prophesied, and took her in his arms again.

Have you missed any of these best-selling Harlequin Romances?

By popular demand... to help complete your collection of Harlequin Romances

50 titles listed on the following pages...

Harlequin Reissues

Harlequin Reissues

Complete and mail this coupon today!